TWAS THE NIGHT

DAN WALSH

BAINBRIDGE PRESS

Twas The Night by Dan Walsh

Bainbridge Press

Editor - Cindi Walsh

ISBN: 978-1-7341417-8-8

Paperback Edition

Copyright © 2022 by Dan Walsh

Cover design by Bainbridge Press

Background Cover photo from 123RF.com:

Image ID: 91287130

Media Type: Stock Photo

Copyright: salajean

❀ Created with Vellum

PROLOGUE

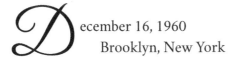ecember 16, 1960
Brooklyn, New York

WHEN THERESA DEMPSEY woke up that morning and took
her first look out the window, she had no idea the view she
was seeing would, shortly and literally, never look the same
again. Nor that the almost-idyllic life she had enjoyed the last
several years with Tom and their two kids, Tommy and
Megan, would likewise be forever changed.

Their street, Sterling Place, looked the same as it ever did,
like every other block in Brooklyn's Park Slope neighborhood. Four-story brownstones up and down the street
converted into four-unit apartments. The first floors had
been turned into little street-front stores specializing in one
thing or another. When they'd moved in three years ago,
Tommy Junior screamed with joy when he saw two candy
stores on their block. A Fanny Farmer's on one corner, and a

Ma and Pa store a few doors down from their place. In the warmer months, it sold homemade ice cream, too.

This block had everything. A nice little grocery store on the other corner, a laundromat above that, a barbershop, and when they could find a babysitter, a bowling alley across the street. Served decent cheeseburgers there, too.

Of course, with the winter storm that had blown through a few days ago, the most glaring thing about the street below were the huge piles of snow lying around everywhere. The center of the street had been cleared but not around the parked cars. Ones that hadn't been driven yet were still completely covered.

A few mornings ago, when the snow had first fallen, the view out this window was actually quite beautiful. Theresa hated how quickly and how ugly it got once the cars, delivery trucks, and buses started plowing through. Now all the edges of the snow piles had turned into dark brown slush. That's what got tracked up the steps, down the hall, and through the front door.

The kids could care less about that. Snow was snow, and they loved everything about it. Tom heard on the radio there was a chance it could snow again closer to Christmas, now only nine days away.

Theresa's gaze shifted to the sky, what she could see of it anyway. Not very pretty. All gray and hazy. And cold looking. She wouldn't be surprised if it snowed a little today. She felt the warm arms of her husband wrap around her from behind.

"Look who finally woke up," he said.

"I know. I never sleep in anymore. Why didn't you wake me?"

"I dunno. Figured since I didn't have to go into work

today, I'd get up with the kids. Give you a break." Tom usually worked on Fridays but took a vacation day, so they could finally get a Christmas tree and set it up. "When I got home last night, I saw those guys selling trees on the street still had a few decent ones left. I asked the main guy if he could hold one for me, but he said not unless I gave him a five-dollar deposit. Didn't have any cash, so I wanted to get down there this morning before they're all gone."

She turned around and gave him a kiss. "You're waiting for the kids, though, right? They'd be so disappointed if—"

"Of course, I'm waiting for them. What, you're not coming with us? Thought we'd make this a family thing."

"I'll go down with you, if you can wait long enough for me to get presentable, maybe grab something to eat."

"Already took care of breakfast," he said. "Kids wanted pancakes. Plenty left for you. But you might want to eat before getting presentable. Pancakes will be cold if you eat after."

He was still close enough to hug, so she hugged him again. "Mmm, warm pancakes with butter and syrup that I didn't have to make? And I got to sleep in? Feels like Mother's Day."

He squeezed her tight then let go. "You deserve it, Babe. Go on, eat. I'll go shave and get myself *presentable*, so you can have the bathroom."

FORTY MINUTES later and all bundled up, Theresa, Tom, and the kids were out on the sidewalk. Tommy was ten now, so he always led the way. Megan was half his age, so she was holding Mommy's hand. A few doors down, Theresa saw the two men selling Christmas trees. "See," she said to Tom, "you didn't need to rush me. There's no other customers standing by the trees. Everyone else is probably at work. See any of the good ones you were looking at last night?"

"In fact, I do. You were right. You kids ready to get a tree?"

"Yes!" They said in unison.

"Do we get to help pick it out?" Tommy said.

"Sure," said Tom. "We'll decide…together." He looked at her and smiled.

She knew he'd figure a way to get the kids to pick out the one he wanted. Tom was very particular about his Christmas trees.

"Daddy," Megan said, "if we're decorating the tree tonight, we're gonna miss the Flintstones."

Tom looked down. "Honey, the Flintstones don't come on till 8:30. We'll have this tree all finished before then."

"We will?"

"I promise.

Theresa smiled. The kids loved watching TV. They didn't own one yet. Maybe someday. The Hamilton's across the hall had one. Their son was a year younger than Tommy. A few months ago, his folks okayed Tommy's family coming over to watch the Flintstones every Friday night. Soon after, the invitation grew to include The Red Skelton Show—her favorite—and the Beverly Hillbillies.

When they got closer, one of the men selling the trees looked over at them. Tom yelled, "Told you I'd be back."

"Yes, you did. Guessing this is the family?"

"It is. And we're ready to get our tree, aren't we kids?"

"Yes, we are," they both said.

The man walked toward a cluster of trees leaning against a brick wall. "I've got a couple back here I'm sure you'll like."

It looked to Theresa like they only had about a dozen left. "Tom, these aren't the prickly ones, are they?"

"No, they're Douglas Firs. Got soft needles. I checked last night." As he led the kids toward the man, he whispered, "He knows the ones I like. He's heading right for them."

Theresa looked at her watch. It was 10:25. "I'll tell you what. You guys pick out a good one. I'm going down to the corner store for a few minutes to get a few goodies we can eat tonight while we decorate." She looked at Tom. "You got the money out of the jar, right?"

He patted his back pocket. "Right here. You go ahead and get what you need to." He leaned over, gave her a quick kiss. She started to walk toward the store. "Hey, if they got any eggnog, get some."

She smiled. It wouldn't be Christmas for Tom without eggnog.

As she walked away, he yelled, "And be careful on that sidewalk. Watch out for the icy spots."

"I will."

When she got to the corner store, a middle-aged man was coming out. He was nice enough to hold the door open. "Thanks."

"Merry Christmas," he said then walked to the intersection.

She stepped inside, relieved to feel the heat. As the door closed, she pulled her list out from her pocket and looked it over. She'd been here so many times she knew where everything was, except the holiday stuff. Maybe she'd better ask about the eggnog first, since it wasn't on her list. "Say, Mr. Sawyer. How ya doin' this morning?"

"Very well, Terry. How 'bout you?"

She'd given up reminding him her name was Theresa

sometime last year. "Just fine. Tom and the kids are down with those two guys selling trees, picking one out. Setting it up tonight."

"That'll be fun. I miss doin' that."

"You and your wife don't set one up anymore?"

"We do. A little one. But it's not as fun without the kids. Course, ours got kids of their own. Least they live nearby, so we'll get to see them Christmas day. Looking for anything in particular?"

"Yeah. Got any eggnog?"

"Should have a few quarts left, over in that case where I keep the cold sodas."

"Great," she said, "my Tom—"

Suddenly, they both froze and looked up. A very loud and very strange noise.

"What is that?" Mr. Sawyer said.

A second later, the same noise but ten times louder. Felt like it was coming right at them, right through the ceiling. They ducked. Then a loud crashing, crunching sound. The whole building rumbled and shook. A massive explosion behind them, in the direction of her house, louder than anything she'd ever heard. The building continued shaking, everything started falling off the shelves. Felt like the walls were gonna come down right on top of them. She screamed as some invisible force slammed her against the counter. She hit her head and saw stars.

Just before she blacked out, she said aloud, "Tom...the kids..."

CHAPTER 1

*T*WO YEARS LATER
Deep in the North Carolina Woods

SAKES ALIVE, but it was cold out here. Ransom couldn't even feel his toes no more. And the sun had already set over the hills, not that you could see it much through all these trees. But it meant the temperature was gonna drop even worse. He'd better gather up the rest of this firewood and skedaddle back to the cabin quick as he could. What made it doubly hard was having to carry this rifle at the ready. Pa had made a rucksack slung over his shoulders to carry the wood in, so Ransom's hands would be free for the gun. His last words before Ransom headed out was, "*You keep them eyes peeled for wolves. Food's been scarce for us and for them. Don't you be their next meal. They even meaner when they're hungry.*"

Then he got to coughing again and had to lay down.

Ransom had to stop a minute, catch his breath. Almost wished he could lay down. What with the cold, the weight of the gun, the sack of wood, and traipsin' around these hills...it was taking its toll. These days with Pa being sick, it fell on him to do all his chores and Pa's, which included the hunting. They usually still got the firewood together, though. His dad would carry the gun along with a rucksack twice the size of the one he'd made Ransom. After a couple of hours, between 'em, they'd get enough wood to last three days.

Ransom hoped he'd be able to at least get enough to keep the cabin warm through the night, maybe some left over to cook breakfast.

He turned around and examined the ground behind him, made sure he could still see his footprints in the fading light. It hadn't snowed in about a week, but there was still a few inches that hadn't melted away. Yeah, he could still see his tracks. Should be okay at least a few minutes more. That was one of the problems living in the same spot in the woods for so many years. Had to keep venturing out farther and farther to find enough good wood laying around on the ground.

A month ago, it didn't matter so much. Pa had himself a real good axe. Same one he'd used to build their cabin. They needed more wood, he'd just chop down a tree. Ransom would just get sent out to gather up some kindling every now and then. If it weren't too cold out, he'd bring his little sister, Emma, along with him. She was six. She'd get maybe a few handfuls of twigs before she'd get distracted by something, then be more trouble than she was worth till they got home.

But that was before Pa's axe broke in two. Beyond mending, Pa had said. "Have to get a new one somehow." But Ransom knew...that'd mean traveling for miles to where the nearest city folks lived. He'd never actually seen any of them before. Pa kept sayin' one day he'd take both he and Emma there, but he never did.

Now he was too sick to go anywhere.

Ransom reached the top of a familiar hill and decided to start heading back. He walked about ten paces to his left, enough to where he could still see his footprints, but far enough to where he might find some decent pieces he'd missed on the way here. He wasn't but fifteen yards down the hill when he suddenly stopped. Felt sure he'd just heard a low growl. Came from his right. He squatted down and cocked his rifle, stared at some nearby bushes where he thought the growling came from.

Couldn't say for sure yet what it was, but —there it was again. Some kind of animal growling just beyond that bush. Couldn't tell if it was a wolf. Could be, but almost sounded like something else. How he hoped it was something else.

Something much smaller.

He moved a few steps toward where he'd been heading. It growled again. This time he was sure it *wasn't* a wolf. Maybe a badger or a wolverine. Either one would make for good eating, 'specially since their meat supply was nearly gone. Course, Pa said a badger got hold of your leg, they'd tear it up something fierce. Out here with no medicine, a wound like that might get green in it, have to get lopped off. But afore that, you might just freeze to death. If it did get the better of him, who'd come out to save him? No one would even know. He was too far out to be heard from the cabin, and even if he did get heard, Pa was too sick to come after him.

No, he better back off, go on his way. It was getting too dark and too cold to take such chances. But after he got about twenty paces away, he took out Pa's Bowie knife and made an arrow symbol in a tree, pointing toward the

animal. Maybe he could come back here for it in the morning when the odds were more in his favor, do some tracking.

THIRTY MINUTES LATER, it was too dark to see his footprints anymore. But Ransom knew where he was now. Sadly, it was on account of his Pa's coughing. Sounded even worse than it did this morning. He hurried fast as he could, given the weight he had in tow.

When he could see the cabin through the trees, he yelled out, "It's me, Pa. I'm back." He could see how dim the light was coming through the windows. Meant the fireplace was either burned out or close to it. That meant the cabin had to be cold as ice. Pa's sickness would get even worse. "I'm coming."

Somehow, he found the strength to run the last fifty feet.

Emma rushed out the door to meet him. "I tried Ransom, but the fire went out. The wood's all gone. I poked and poked, but it just went out."

"That's okay, Emma. Don't fret. I'll get it blazin' hot in no time. Go get our blankets off our bed and put 'em on top of Pa till I fix things."

"Already done that."

"Good girl." He walked up the small front porch and through the front door. "Then you can help me get this fire goin'." He looked over at his father, just a lump in the shadows over by the corner. "I'll have you warmed up in no time, Pa. You'll see."

"I know you will, son," Pa said weakly.

"Don't be talkin' now. Gotta reserve your strength. You drinkin' water? You always tell me how much I gotta drink when I'm sick."

"It's all out," he said. "Pitcher's empty."

"That's what you can do, Emma. Get Pa some fresh water."

She looked up at him, tears suddenly in her eyes.

"What's the matter?"

"I tried to keep his glass filled, but when the fire went out, the pitcher froze. It ain't empty. It just froze."

"That's okay. Go on and bring it over here. We'll set it close to the fire, soon as I get this lit. That'll be your job. To watch and see when enough melts to fill up his glass. The rest will melt in no time."

"Okay," she said.

Pa coughed again. Ransom gave her a quick hug, then set to work building the fire.

In less than ten minutes, it was going right nicely. He was already warming up enough to feel his toes again. "We'll get that fire to reach you in a few more minutes, Pa. You think if I helped you, you could come over here and sit in this chair by the fire? You know, with them blankets still on?"

After coughing some more, Pa said, "Don't think I can, son."

"I think I can pour him some water now," Emma said.

"Good. You do that." Looking at Pa. "You drink that water, Pa. I'll put some drier pieces on this fire, and we'll be all set."

Just as Ransom finished adding the next round of wood to the fire, Pa said in a gravelly voice, "You did real good, son. Real good. I get some more water in me, get warmed up a bit, I'll need you to come over here close to me, so we can talk.

Got some important words I gotta speak to you. Some things I been needing to say for quite a spell."

Ransom sighed. Didn't know what Pa could be meaning by that, but a feeling of dread suddenly pressed down on his chest.

CHAPTER 2

*B*lack Rock, North Carolina

"Say, Bud. You hear someone finally bought that old Hansen place over on Elk Hill Road?"

Deputy Ellison "Bud" Wallace finished buckling his gun holster, looked over at his boss, Sheriff Andy Rickards. "Think that's old news, Andy. That happened over a month ago. Read it in the Sunday papers. Nobody's moved in yet. Drove by there yesterday. Someone's done some work on it, though. Yard looks all picked up. Saw a big pile of dead branches out by the road."

Andy had his feet up on his desk, like he did most mornings. At least till he finished his first cup of coffee. "Well, maybe I heard it wrong then. Guess the *new* news is…somebody's finally moving in. A big truck was seen riding through town first thing this morning, heading that way. Ain't no one

moved into Black Rock in over a year. Guess it got folks'
attention."

Bud walked over to his desk in the corner. "How'd you
know it rode all the way out to the Hansen place?"

"An eyewitness reported back to me."

Bud smiled. "An eyewitness, eh? This truck engage in any
suspicious activity?"

Andy laughed, playing along. "Unfortunately, no.
Appeared to be only interested in delivering furniture and
such to the aforementioned premises."

Bud grabbed his mug, headed over to the pot. "And who
was this eyewitness?"

"Margie. Of course, she kept her distance, so as not to
appear nosy. She did say it was puzzling, though, seeing how
small the truck was compared to how big the Hansen
place is."

Margie was the other employee at the Sheriff's office. A
civilian, as Andy sometimes liked to say. She answered the
phone, typed the occasional letter, did filing when it needed
doing, kept the coffeepot fresh all day and, of course, kept
Andy and Bud informed of all the goings-on in town. And
they had her to thank for all the Christmas decorations
adorning the Sheriff's office.

Bud filled his mug, started adding the sugar. "Well, guess
we won't be calling it the old Hansen place anymore. She see
who was moving in? That article in the paper didn't say. Just
that the new owner was coming down from New York, of all
places."

Andy took his feet off the desk, leaned forward in his
chair. "Well, that's where the story gets interesting. Margie
said—"

Just then, the main door opened and in walked Margie,

carrying the mail. She worked in a small outer office, something of a reception area.

"Well," Andy said, "I'll let her tell you herself. Margie, tell Bud what you observed as you surveilled the old Hansen place this morning."

She made a face. "I wasn't *surveilling*. I was just...curious. Obviously, you two gentlemen are just as curious, or you wouldn't be asking about it first thing."

"She's got a point," Bud said. He genuinely was curious. Probably on account of how little anything ever changed in Black Rock, day to day. "So, what'd you see. Who's moving in?"

She set the mail down on Andy's desk. "Well, at first I didn't see anyone but the movers. Someone had to be there, I knew. Else, how would they get in? But they did, and I watched to see what kind of stuff they were bringing down the ramp. Whoever it is, they gotta have money. For starters, that Hansen place — like all the homes on that road — are big as mansions, compared to the homes most folks live in. And all the furniture I did see them carrying looked brand-new."

"Margie," Andy said, "how could you tell the furniture was new if you — as previously reported — kept your distance?"

Bud laughed. Andy loved talking like this, like some kind of courthouse lawyer. Started doing it about a year ago, after he bought his first TV and started watching Perry Mason.

"Well," Margie said, "I got good eyes. Besides, a woman knows when she's looking at new furniture. And this stuff was nice, not like the kind of stuff you buy around here. Like the stores if you drive all the way to Asheville, but—"

"Get to the good part, Margie. When you got a glimpse of

the lady of the house." Andy looked at Bud. "Pay attention now, son."

Bud hated it when Andy called him *son*. He was maybe ten years older.

Margie looked at Bud. "Not sure why Andy's calling this the good part. But I finally did see a very attractive young lady come out at some point and talk to one of the delivery men. A brunette. Far as I could tell, she was there alone. Never saw a man, like a husband. Never saw any kids."

"Well," Bud said, "maybe her husband and their kids haven't arrived yet. Maybe she came in a little early to get the house set up." He knew what the two of them were getting at. They were always trying to fix him up with somebody, convinced *a fine looking young man his age*, as Margie put it, should already be married and have a couple of young-uns.

"I don't think so," Margie said. "What kind of husband would send his wife down early to do all that work by herself?"

"I don't know. Guess not a very good one. But what kind of young attractive woman with no husband or kids buys a great big place like that? To live in all by herself?"

Margie looked stumped. She looked at Andy then back at Bud. "Hadn't thought about that. That is rather unusual, I'll give you that."

Andy put his feet back up on his desk. "The plot thickens." He looked over at Bud. "Guess you'll have to drive on out there and investigate the situation for yourself."

"Andy, there is no situation to investigate."

"Well," Margie said, "how about I make a nice plate of gingerbread cookies? I could bring them in tomorrow, and you could take them out there to her? You know, welcome her into town?"

Bud shook his head. "You two gotta stop. I'll find myself the right girl when the time's right."

"What girl?" Margie said. "Most of the nicer ones are already married, the ones who aren't moved off to Asheville where the prospects are a tad better than here."

Bud knew, she was only exaggerating a little. Eight years ago, the girl he'd loved since high school did that very thing. Found herself a young, ambitious fella in Asheville, whom she admitted she didn't love. But he did wind up getting her what she craved more: bundles of money, a fine car, beautiful clothes, and a big house. Not the kind of life Bud could afford as a deputy in a town like Black Rock.

"Whatta you say?" said Andy. "I could turn Margie loose for a few hours to make those cookies now. She could have them back here by midafternoon."

Bud stood. Walked over to the rack and grabbed his hat and coat. "Think I'll do what the good folks of Black Rock are paying me to do. Drive on over to the other side of town and follow up on that call we got thirty minutes ago."

"You mean the one from Buster Sims," Andy said. "About that noise ordinance infraction? I'm telling you, there's nothing to it. I was out there a few days ago. It's just his neighbor's kid practicing his trumpet for the Christmas school play. I told him he needed to lighten up, stop being such a Scrooge."

"Well, I took the call and said I'd come out there and check."

"Do that, if you must," Andy said. "After that, if I were you, I'd take a drive to the north side of town, do a little patrolling along Elk Hill Road. Show that nice young lady from New York a little southern hospitality."

CHAPTER 3

eep in the North Carolina Woods

IT HAD BEEN a bitter cold night in that cabin, but Ransom did the best he could keeping the fire fed. At least, Emma slept through. And sounded like, for the most part, Pa did too. But between Pa's coughing fits and working that fire, Ransom was plumb tuckered out. That was okay. He'd get caught up on his rest today. Except for going out later to gather some more firewood, he had no other chores.

He felt a tug on his coat, turned around to see Emma had woken up.

"Will you be getting my breakfast again?"

"Sorry to tell ya, all we got is what's left over from last night. Should be okay to eat, though. Don't think it got cold enough to freeze in here. You could warm it up by the fire."

She pouted but quickly recovered. "All right then. Want me to get it for myself?"

Pa started coughing again. Ransom could tell by the sound of it, it was gonna be a bad one. "Guess you better. I need to check on Pa." He got up quickly, went over to check on Pa's water glass. It was empty. "I'll get this filled right quick, Pa. Want me to help you sit up a little?"

"Would you, son? Maybe just a little."

After doing that, Ransom fetched the water. "Here, take a drink. It's ice cold. Want me to heat it by the fire, warm it up some?"

"No. Maybe the cold water will tamp down this fire in my throat." He coughed some more. After taking a few sips, he glanced over at Emma by the fireplace. Quietly he said, "Ransom, we need to have that talk I spoke about last night. I need to say some things ain't fit for Emma's ears. Fact is, wish you didn't need to hear them neither. But..." He coughed some more. "They need to be said. And it's too cold to send her outside."

Ransom looked over at Emma. "Got an idea, Pa. I'll take care of it and be right back." He hurried over to a wooden storage box at the foot of his bed. Didn't take long to find the two knit caps Ma had made them before she died. She would've wanted them to be worn every winter, starting with the first one after she passed. But Ransom couldn't bring himself to use 'em, afraid they'd wear out, and he'd have nothing left from her if they did. He brought them over to Emma.

She saw what he was holding. "What are you gonna do with those? Thought you said they were special, so we couldn't wear 'em."

"I know, Emma. But this is a special time. Pa needs to talk to me, and..." He had to think of something to say that wouldn't get her scared as he was about what Pa had to say. "...And I need to make sure you're warm while we talk."

"How long you be talking with Pa?"

"Hopefully, not long." He put both caps on her head, folded them so they'd be double-thick over her ears. Then he went back to check on Pa. When he got close, Ransom got quite a fright. Pa's eyes were closed, and he wasn't coughing. "Oh Lord, no," he whispered. When he bent down to see if he was breathing, Pa woke up coughing.

He was so relieved.

Pa looked over at Emma. "That's good thinking, son. That's at least one small comfort. You got your mother's smarts."

"You're plenty smart, Pa. Everything I know, I learned from you. But you got lots more to teach me, so you...you got to get —" Ransom started choking up.

"Look at me, son."

He did. Tried to get control of himself.

"Ransom, you need to know. I won't be getting better."

"Pa, don't say—"

"Hush now, son. I don't have the strength to wrestle words with you. Same thing's happening to me happened to your Ma three winters ago. I know. I'm the one tried to get her better. But I can tell, I'm at the same place she was when she was...near the end. Might be today, might be tomorrow. Feel I'm ready to see her again. Hope I'm as ready to meet Jesus."

Tears flowed down Ransom's cheeks. Pa needed to stop talking like this. He glanced over at Emma. She'd finished eating and was now playing with a doll Ma had made her. Like everything was just fine as it could be.

"Should've told you these things long before now but

never seemed to find the time. But you need to know who you are, son, who your people are, and how we come — your Ma and me — to be in this cabin, living out here all these years by ourselves. You especially need to know what I want you and Emma to do once I'm gone."

Over the next hour, stopping only to cough or take sips of cold water, Pa told him one tale after another. Things he'd never heard told before. Many of them things Ransom had longed to know about but never dared ask. The way things were set up, he knew it weren't never his place. But now here was Pa telling him answers to all those things and a bunch more things Ransom never thought to ask.

He learned he was actually part of a great big clan of folks who lived in a holler almost a hundred miles from here, nestled in the middle of a totally different set of mountains. His Ma's folks lived in a different holler about a day's horse ride from Pa's. His grandpa owned tons of land, and his whole family worked every day sawing down trees. They worked with a lumber mill owned by Ma's family, until there had been a terrible falling out.

Problem was, Ransom's Pa and Ma had grown up loving each other and were fixing to get married soon as they were old enough. Been planning this from the time they'd started grade school and first learned how to read. Until that moment, Ransom didn't even know Pa *could* read. Pa went on to say how sorry he was that neither he nor Emma ever got taught. It was always his Ma's plan to teach them, but after she died, Pa was too busy hunting and doing all the chores to ever get to it. At this point, Pa actually had tears in his eyes but quickly wiped them away.

Well, next he said that this falling out between their families got worse and worse. It spread throughout both hollers, with lots of fights and bad feelings, and even some blood was shed. Ransom had many questions about this but Pa said he didn't have the strength to go there. Suffice it to say, he and Ma were forbidden to marry, or even bring up the subject ever again.

So, they ran away, far away, until they knew both families had stopped chasing them. Found a preacher to marry them and wound up settling here in these hills where they built this cabin. They had only meant for it to be for a year, maybe two. Their plan had always been to make their way to the nearest town, start living the kind of life city folks do.

But that never happened.

It was supposed to. Pa stressed this. And now, especially now, he was terrible sorry it never did. Then came the last part of Pa's tale. He wanted to say more but Ransom could tell, he didn't have the strength. But before he said it, he made Ransom take hold of both hands, look him straight in the eyes, and make him promise…that when the time came for him to go be with their Ma, Ransom would do what Pa should've done long ago.

He told Ransom he was *not* to go back where they came from, not to try and find their family on either side. Not until he and Emma were full grown. He made Ransom promise he'd take his sister, and the two of them would make their way to the nearest town—somewhere well south of here—find some nice church people he could tell his story to. See if they could put them with other folks who'd raise them right. And he needed to make them church folks promise— and he stressed this was the thing that mattered most—to never let anyone split him and Emma apart.

CHAPTER 4

lack Rock, North Carolina

THIS MIGHT JUST BE the most peculiar day Theresa had ever had.

She was walking with the supervisor of this moving crew through both floors of this big new house holding a clipboard, checking off all the boxes and furniture pieces they had just delivered, making sure they were all here, and all put in their proper place. That last part was the most important, because after they left she'd be here all by herself, no one to help her lift these heavy things and put them somewhere else.

"Well, Robert," she said, looking at the name tag on his jumpsuit, "looks like they're all here." She handed him back the clipboard after signing at the bottom and attaching a ten-dollar bill to it. "Here's a little tip for you to share with your crew. Thank them for me for getting everything here on time and all loaded in here without any damage."

Robert took the clipboard, quickly removed and pocketed the money. "Why, thank you, Mrs. Dempsey. You didn't have to do that, but it's much appreciated. The boys and I will sure be eating well tonight. Now you're certain you got everything where you want it, especially like that couch and that hutch. I don't expect a little lady like you could move things like that a few inches, let alone into another room."

Theresa kept walking Robert toward the front door. The rest of his crew were already in the truck. "Pretty sure things are where they need to be. If not, won't be a problem. Got all kinds of family coming down from up north tomorrow. They'll help me if anything needs moving."

"Oh, I see." He opened the front door. "I could tell you had a northern accent, but I'm not too good at picking out one from the other."

"I'm from New York City, born and raised in Brooklyn."

"Like where the Dodgers play?" he said.

"Not quite," Theresa said. "Guess you're not much of a baseball fan. The Dodgers moved out to Los Angeles five years ago. They used to play in Brooklyn but not anymore. We have the New York Mets playing in New York now, but not in Brooklyn where I'm from."

"Naw," Robert said. "Don't follow baseball much. Football's more my game." He stepped outside, buttoned up his coat. "Man, seems like it's ten degrees colder than when we started unloading this truck. Okay then, you have a nice day and hope you and your family have a Merry Christmas."

"Thank you. Better get this door closed before all that cold air blows in." She walked back into the big foyer. The left side opened to a huge living room, bigger than her entire apartment back in Brooklyn. On the right, was a formal dining room. Until now, the kind she had only ever seen in movies. In front of her was a wide stairwell leading up to the second floor.

Exhausted, she sat on one of the lower steps. She'd already turned the heat up several degrees but wondered if she might need to light that big stone fireplace, as well.

Who was she kidding? She had never built a fire in a fireplace before. The real estate man was kind enough to have someone cut up a whole bunch of firewood for her, all different sizes. Stored most of it in a rack outside but left a nice pile for her right by the fireplace. It probably never dawned on him someone from Brooklyn wouldn't know what to do next.

You and your family have a Merry Christmas.

Robert's last words replayed in her mind.

She inhaled deeply, exhaled an even deeper sigh. There was no family coming from up north tomorrow. And certainly none coming for Christmas. She'd only said that to quiet a fear in her own heart. She didn't like the idea of all those men knowing she'd be in this house all by herself.

She looked around at everything her eyes could take in from this stairwell. What was she doing here? Had she really just bought this big place…for just her? When the realtor had first shown it to her a few weeks back, she was positive it was easily as big as the brownstone they had lived in back home. And that place housed four apartments. Four different families taking up the same space. And all of them were just renting from a landlord. None of them ever had expectations of ever buying their own place. That was something rich people did.

Well, she never had an expectation of them buying their

own place, either, but Tom did. He'd always said that one day they'd move out of Brooklyn and find themselves a nice place in that beautiful little town west of Asheville, North Carolina, where they had spent their honeymoon. Tom had always wanted to see the mountains and surprised her with plans to drive down there after the wedding. She had always figured they'd honeymoon in Niagara Falls where most of their friends had.

But Tom had read this article in *Look Magazine* about this huge mansion called The Biltmore Estate near Asheville. The article said that it was owned by the famous Vanderbilt family, and that they'd started opening it up for people to tour through. Tom decided they'd go there, see the Biltmore, and drive around a few days, take in all that fresh mountain air and beautiful scenery.

Walking through the Biltmore was amazing, but even more so, was the drive they took the day after. They wound up eating lunch at a diner in a charming little town, called Black Rock. Both were instantly smitten with the place. They walked all over then drove through several neighborhoods, dreaming about what it must be like to live there. So quiet. So uncrowded. So many beautiful trees. Clean streets and houses with their own yards.

By the end of the day when it was time to head back to their hotel in Asheville, Tom had declared, "One day, my love, we're gonna come back here, buy ourselves a nice house, and raise a family."

Remembering this moment now, caused her eyes to well up in tears. "Well, Tom. Here I am. I finally made it to that little town you loved. And we certainly have a nice house." Way bigger than either of them dared to dream. But Tom wasn't there to share it with her. Neither was Tommy, nor Megan.

They were in heaven with Jesus. Almost two years ago to the day.

That's what that horribly loud and noisy explosion had been about on Sterling Place that morning. The one that had shaken all the merchandise off Mr. Sawyer's store shelves and had thrown her head against the counter, knocking her unconscious.

Moments before, high in the sky, two airplanes had collided, sending both of them hurling toward the ground. One of them fell on Staten Island. The other had fallen on top of them, their perfect little neighborhood of Park Slope in Brooklyn, killing all one hundred and twenty-eight passengers and crew, as well as six people on the ground.

Including, the two men selling Christmas trees. And including her Tom, little Tommy, and her precious Megan.

CHAPTER 5

*A*bout thirty minutes ago, Deputy Bud Wallace finished up with Buster Simms and his noise complaint. It was like Andy had said. Buster was sick and tired of that neighbor kid wailing away on the trumpet. Bud wasn't sure what else Andy had said besides *stop being such a Scrooge.* He pointed out to Buster that the good folks governing Black Rock hadn't seen fit to create any laws forbidding children from learning how to play musical instruments. Him not liking something didn't make it illegal, so Bud was powerless to do anything to try to make him stop.

As Bud listened, he got Buster to admit the kid didn't practice early in the morning or late at night. As far as Bud could tell, he'd practiced for a reasonable length of time and at normal times of the day. So, Bud recommended Buster get him a nice pair of earplugs, maybe a comfortable pair of headphones to cut down on the noise.

For the last few minutes, Bud sat in his squad car pulled just off the side of the road under a big billboard. It was out on the northern edge of town, near where a major state road came through. Everyone who lived in Black Rock knew the speed limit dropped from 55mph to 35 right after this billboard. But motorists from out of town often didn't see the signs warning them to slow down, and they'd barrel down this road like moonshiners on a run. Andy liked him to spend at least a few hours out here, at different times of the day, to discourage that sort of thing. If folks were going too fast, Bud would chase after them and give them a ticket.

In Black Rock, driving too fast and playing your trumpet too loud were about as dangerous as things got.

Just then, a big black Chevy came hauling down the road in Bud's direction. Bud recognized it. Bobby Robbins, a spoiled high school kid who lived nearby. Sure enough, once he saw Bud's squad car he slammed on the brakes, then whipped his car to the right, fishtailing as he tried to make the turn onto Elk Hill Road. He straightened out and got back in his own lane as he rode off. Technically, Bobby wasn't speeding but that did seem reckless enough for Bud to give him at least the threat of a ticket.

Bud turned on his lights but not the siren and took off after him. Bobby had maybe a two-block head start, but he wasn't speeding so Bud caught up with him fairly quickly. In fact, Bobby pulled over right in front of the old Hansen place. The one Andy and Margie were yakking about that morning. The one where — according to Margie — *an attractive young brunette* had just moved in.

As Bud walked up to the driver-side window, he saw Bobby shaking his head back and forth. When he was standing right next to him, Bobby said, "Ah, c'mon Bud. You're not gonna give me a ticket for that, are ya? I slowed down soon as I saw you. My turn was a little rough, but nobody was coming the other way, so nothing bad happened."

"First of all, Bobby. You're still in high school. You don't get to call me Bud. It's Deputy Wallace, all right?"

"Sorry...*Deputy* Wallace."

"Second thing is, yeah, you slowed down as soon as you saw me. But what if I hadn't been there? Fast as you were going, your car could've flipped over on that turn. I see you're not wearing a seatbelt—"

"No law against that."

"No, there's not. But what kind of shape would you be in if your car flipped over in some ditch? And lastly, what if someone *had* been coming down Elk Hill Road going the other way? There's at least a dozen houses on this road. The two of you would've smacked into each other head on."

"Okay, okay. I get it. I should-a slowed down way before seeing you on the side of the road. But can you give me a break this time? My dad said one more ticket, and he locks up my car for a month."

"This time?" Bud said. "I seem to recall I gave you a break the last time. What was that, not even two weeks ago? Afraid I can't this time, Bobby." He took out his ticket pad and pen. Right after that, Bobby did something Bud did not expect.

He started crying. First time Bud had ever seen any other emotion at work inside Bobby besides anger. Maybe he was being serious about being willing to change. He put the pad away. "Okay, Bobby. This is your last break. I'm serious. You better start driving around Black Rock like a little old lady."

"I will, Bud — I mean, Deputy Wallace. Honest, I'll straighten out."

Something off in the distance caught Bud's eye. He looked over the hood and saw that young brunette inside the

Hansen place standing by the front window looking their way. He glanced down at Bobby. "I'm gonna hold you to it, Bobby. Now, go on. Head on home. Slowly." Bobby's folks' place was about three houses away from here. But Elk Hill was a winding road and the properties were spaced far apart, so you couldn't see it from here.

As Bobby drove off, Bud looked to see…the young woman was still watching. He waved as he walked back to his car. She waved back and moved away from the window. Hard to tell from here, but *attractive* might be too weak a word to describe her.

She was beautiful.

Could she really be living in such a big house like this…all by herself?

Maybe, since he was here, he should stop in and say hello.

He leaned into the car, turned off the blinking lights, remembered Margie's offer to make gingerbread cookies. Now, he kinda wished he'd taken her up on that.

CHAPTER 6

his wasn't the kind of thing Theresa wanted to see barely half a day at her new place. A police car with his lights flashing on the street right out by her house. Looked like the cop pulled over someone driving a shiny black Chevy. She'd seen more than her share of police incidents back in Brooklyn, thought coming here would be the end of that.

As she studied the situation further, though, it didn't seem all that sinister. Nobody was pulling any guns out, getting patted down, or shoved into the back of the squad car. The distance to the street was a good stretch, but from what she could see, the cop had kept a mostly pleasant look on his face.

Whatever it was, it seemed to be over. The driver of the Chevy was driving off, nice and slow. Uh-oh, the cop was looking this way. Now, he waved. What should she do? It would be rude just to close the curtains. She waved back.

Then she closed the curtains.

Well, that was different. As a rule, cops in Brooklyn didn't smile and wave. The pot of coffee she set up in the new percolator should be ready by now. She was heading toward the kitchen and just about there when the doorbell rang. It made her jump. Who could it be? Maybe the cop? She wasn't expecting anyone else today. She couldn't even see her nearest neighbor, didn't figure anyone would be carrying over a pie or some other housewarming gift.

She looked through the peephole in the front door. She'd always wanted one of these things.

Oh my gosh, it was the cop.

She stood back from the door, not sure what to do. Of course, she had to open it. But what should she say? She never talked to cops. If they ever had a reason to get close to one, Tom did all the talking.

"Just a second," she yelled through the door.

"That's okay, Ma'am. Don't mean to bother you."

He sounded harmless. And he called her *Ma'am*. No one ever called her Ma'am. Maybe, *Hey Lady*. She looked through the peephole again, just for a second. Did he think she was old, calling her Ma'am? He looked about the same age as her.

"Is everything okay?" he asked.

She was being ridiculous. She took a deep breath and opened the door. It was freezing out. "Guess you better come inside if we need to talk. I don't have a coat on."

"Okay, then," he said, stomping his shoes on the porch. "Don't want to drag any mud inside."

"I bought a welcome mat," she said. "But I don't know which box it's in." As he crossed the threshold, she closed the door.

He looked around, noticed the stacks of boxes. "Guess you're just moving in?"

"Yeah, today in fact. The truck just left a little while ago."

"Suppose you got a lot of work to do," he said. "Don't want to take too much of your time. Realized, probably wasn't a great first impression of our town, seeing a squad car with its lights flashing right in front of your house. Thought I'd just stop in, say hello, let you know that's not the kind of thing that happens very often around here. At least, not on Elk Hill Road."

"That's kind of you. You said *on Elk Hill Road*. It happen a lot on other roads in town?"

He laughed. "No, that's not what I meant. I was just pulling over a kid who lives a few doors down on this street, on a traffic thing. This really is a safe town. I've been a deputy sheriff here for over eight years, and I can count on one hand the times I pulled out my gun. And all of those were scaring away wild animals."

Now, she laughed. "I'm glad to hear it." She thought a moment. "You get many wild animals?"

"Just every now and then. Like I said," he held up his hand. "I can count the times I had to chase them off on one hand. Of course, your place here is right on the edge of town. Butts right up against those thick, hilly woods. When it gets warm, folks on this road will sometimes see small animals come out, like raccoons and possums."

"But no…mountain lions or bears?"

"No, don't think you have to worry about that. I'm sure you go deep enough in those woods, you might run across critters like that. But they don't come out this way."

The more he talked, the safer she felt. "Well, Sheriff. My name is Theresa. Theresa Dempsey." She held out her hand.

He shook it. "Well, I'm just a Deputy. The full name is Ellison Wallace, but folks in town just call me, Bud. Nice to meet you, Theresa."

"Listen...Bud, I was just gonna pour myself a cup of coffee. You want some?"

Bud looked at his watch. "Can't stay too long, but yeah, weather this cold, I won't turn down a hot cup of coffee."

"Follow me." Theresa walked on the left side of the big stairwell, which led toward the back of the house, where her humongous kitchen was located.

"You sure you don't mind? I don't want to keep you from all your—"

"All my work?" She smiled, then turned right through the kitchen doorway. "It's gonna take me weeks to get to the end of my chore list. I'm happy to have some company." She instantly regretted saying that. Felt it made her sound desperate and lonely.

She was, but that was supposed to be a secret.

As she poured their coffee, got out the creamer from the fridge and bowl of sugar, she noticed him looking all around the kitchen.

"Always wondered what this place looked like inside," he said.

"You've never been in here then? The real estate lady called it the *old Hansen place,* sounded like something everybody in town knew about."

He finished fixing his coffee. "Well, if I'm being honest...I knew you were moving in here today. Well, that *someone* was moving in here today. The whole town pretty much knows. That's something that'll probably take some getting used to, I imagine. Small town curiosity and gossip. When not much happens, little things can become big deals. This place has been empty since old man Hansen died five years ago."

"Guess that explains why it took the cleaning crew over a week to get it in shape." She took a sip of coffee. "So, what's the town saying about me? Heard anything being tossed about? Whatever it is, it's all guesswork, since you're the first person in town I've really talked to." The realtor Theresa had dealt with lived in Asheville.

He smiled. "I'd have to be doing some guessing myself about that, since I do my best to avoid that sort of thing. But I did hear one woman I know trying to figure out if you're the forerunner of a big family to come, or if you're living in this big old place by yourself."

Theresa was a little taken aback to hear this, that she would be the object of the entire town's interest. She hadn't counted on that. She was hoping just to live here in quiet obscurity, minding her own business, and being left mostly alone.

Bud seemed to sense her apprehension to open up and quickly added, "Hey, listen. You don't have to answer that. You just asked what folks might be saying. You don't have to tell me a thing. And anything you did tell me? Well, I'd never tell a soul, unless for some reason you asked me to."

She could tell he meant it. "Thanks, Bud. I appreciate that. That makes you the kind of person I probably wouldn't mind telling my story to. Unfortunately, it'd take way more than one cup of coffee to tell it." She took another sip. "And I gotta figure out — since I moved here and hope to stay a while — whether I want to keep folks guessing about *that young lady who took over the old Hansen place*, or have you send me the best gossip in town and give her the whole kit and caboodle."

Bud laughed. "I think the hardest part of the assignment might be…picking out the best. We've got quite a team of blue-ribbon, award-winning gossips here in Black Rock."

Theresa smiled. Bud was good medicine for the kind of day she'd been having. She was glad he was the first person in town she'd met. "Well, Deputy Wallace, I will give you one piece of information you can officially begin to disseminate. I'm sure it's at the top of quite a few lists. The answer is…Yes, I really did buy this place myself and plan to live in it all by myself. I don't have any big family coming to share it with me, or really, any family at all."

She didn't mean to say that last part. Instantly, she started tearing up. Which surprised her. She'd cried a million tears over the last two years and thought she had finally reached the end of it.

"I'm sorry, Theresa," Bud said quietly. He saw a roll of paper towels on the counter, got up, and gave her one. He was still standing. "You don't have to say anymore. I really appreciate the coffee. I'll give you some space."

"No, that's okay." She wiped her eyes. "You don't have to go, not on account of me anyway. If you got a couple of minutes, I'll give you the short version of what a girl like me is doing in a place like this. I don't mean this big house, although that's part of it. I mean why a girl from Brooklyn is living in a town like Black Rock…all by herself."

CHAPTER 7

*B*ud wound up visiting with Theresa Dempsey for almost thirty minutes, finished a second cup of coffee. She did most of the talking, seemed like it was doing her some good to share these things with someone who wasn't family. He'd learned that was at least part of the reason why she'd decided to leave Brooklyn, where she'd lived her whole life till now. She loved her family but felt they'd never let her heal up from the wounds caused by such a loss.

And it had been a terrific loss. Bud couldn't imagine going through something like that.

He really didn't know what to say. Whatever losses he'd experienced on his journey thus far—added together—couldn't hold a candle to even one of the things Theresa had shared. In the end, he figured his loss for words might've been a good thing. She'd said it was the constant outpouring of words from well-wishing family members and nearby neighbors that kept Theresa so tightly tied to her grief. Every time they'd see her, see the sorrow on her face or the sadness in her eyes, they felt compelled to fill the space with comforting words. She said she knew that's what they were intending. But all it did was force all the memories of that tragic day — and the days right after — rushing back to the forefront of her mind.

And with them, came all the pain.

Even if she had been coping relatively well, trying to move forward. Those *comforting words* always backfired. She said it wasn't just the people around her, either. It was the place itself. Everywhere she went in the neighborhood triggered fond memories with either Tom, the kids, or both. Which only reminded her of the gaping holes left in her heart now that they were gone. Not to mention the gaping holes left in the buildings on Sterling Place, totally destroyed by the downed airplane.

Even two years later in the rebuilt buildings, she said there were still vivid reminders of the ghosts they were supposed to replace. She finally had to give up going down to Sterling Place altogether. Physically distancing helped some. But it was no help at all with the people in her life.

Try as they might, they'd never let her forget.

She told Bud she'd confided all this to her pastor two months ago, because she'd heard somewhere that, "guys like him can't tell anyone your secrets." Bud had to suppress a laugh. It was the way she'd said it with that Brooklyn accent. Her pastor was the one who suggested she might have to consider moving away, to go somewhere brand-new, if she wanted a real chance to heal.

That's when Bud had said, "Well, in that way sheriff deputies are like clergy. We can't share people's secrets, either."

She'd looked at him funny then realized he was joking.

She playfully punched him in the arm. But it wasn't flirty. That was one thing Bud realized early on. Theresa Dempsey hadn't come down here to find a man. She had lost the great love of her life. As beautiful as she was, and as easy as she was to be with, he could easily see...she wasn't looking for love.

The last thing she'd said to him before he left was: *I know, Bud, you're not like a pastor or priest. But I'm a pretty good judge of character. I won't tell you how much or how little of my story to tell others. I'll let you decide. You got a good face...and kind eyes. Somehow, I know you won't do me wrong.*

Sitting there now, alone in his squad car in the side parking lot of the Sheriff's office, Bud muttered aloud, "No, Theresa. That's something I will never do."

A loud rapping on his window.

"You asleep in there, Barney?" Followed by a burst of laughter.

Bud looked up at the face of Herman Whitlock, bundled up in an old hunting jacket. Like so many others around town, he found it to be great fun calling Bud, *Barney*, after the *Barney Fife* character on the Andy Griffith Show. It had come out on television a couple years ago to the delight of millions of viewers, and the irritation of small-town sheriff departments throughout the South.

Bud got out of the car. "No, I wasn't sleeping. I was just thinking on something before I headed inside."

"Headed inside to see *who*?" Herman said.

Bud was just about to say it, then realized what Herman was up to.

"Headed inside to see who?" Herman repeated. "Sheriff Andy?" Then another round of laughter. "If he's Andy, then you gotta be Barney, right?"

Bud shook his head as he walked behind his car toward the office. He stopped and looked at Herman. "Don't you ever get tired of the same routine? I've seen the show. It's pretty entertaining. But maybe you heard, it's called the Andy *Griffith* show. Not the Andy Rickards show." He kept walking and was almost to the front door.

Herman followed. "Oh, I know that. I'm just joshing ya. It was on again last night. Funniest show on TV, you ask me. And that Barney Fife? He's the reason why. So, me calling you Barney is really like a compliment. You can see that, right?"

"Well, Herman, I'll make you a deal. You can keep on calling me Barney, just as long as you're okay with me calling you the character on the show you remind me of."

"Which one is that?"

"Otis. From now on, you'll be Otis, and I'll be Barney."

Herman looked confused. "Not sure I remember…which one's Otis?"

Bud opened the door. "You remember Otis. He's the town drunk." Bud walked in, shut the door behind him.

He noticed Margie wasn't at her desk and, as usual, there was no one else in the reception area. The door into the main room where everything happened was open. As he walked through, he saw Margie filing some papers and *Sheriff Andy* sitting at his desk writing something on a pad. Looking around, he had to admit, while the room layout was nothing like the TV show, it did bear an uncomfortable resemblance. This discussion had come up before, shortly after the show had come out. Andy was quick to point out that their two jail cells were against the back wall, not on the left as you came in the door, like on the TV show. And he and Bud's desks were on the opposite side of the room.

"You're right, Andy," Margie kidded. "They're absolutely nothing alike." A smirk on her face.

"Keep it up," Andy replied, then he'd added, "Aunt Bee."

That had pretty much ended the discussion.

"What are you smiling about?" Margie said, jolting Bud into the moment. "Left a report on your desk you forgot to sign."

"Where you been?" said Andy. "Been out to our speed trap? Made the town any money?"

Bud walked to his desk. "As a matter fact, I was out there. Only gave a stern warning to Bobby Robbins for reckless driving."

"I think you've been givin' him a few too many warnings," Andy said. "Think it's time he started feeling the heat…in his wallet."

"Next time he will. But hey, there's something else. Margie, why don't you come over here, so I won't have to yell."

She hurried over. He decided to lead off with the head-line, "Wound up stopping Bobby Robbins out front of the old Hansen place. Got invited in for coffee by that young attractive brunette Margie had seen, the one who just moved in."

The look on their faces was priceless. He had their full and undivided attention. "We talked for almost thirty minutes, in fact. Well mainly, she talked. Telling me where she came from, how she came to move down here from Brooklyn, why she bought the Hansen place, and how she came to have the money to buy it, along with all the new things inside."

"Oh, my goodness," Margie said. "That is so much more than I'd hoped for. So, the two of you hit it off?"

Bud's face grew serious. "In a way, I think we did. But not

the way you're hoping, Margie. In fact, I'm gonna share some of what she told me, and it's gonna be about the saddest story you ever heard. Starting with...you remember those two airplanes that crashed over New York City two Christmases ago? All those poor people who died? Well, one of those planes came down on top of the block where she lived. Her husband and two little children were some of those folks who died."

Margie and Andy's faces quickly shifted at this news. "Oh, my Lord," Margie said.

"I'll tell you some more," Bud said, "but I know you'll agree with me when you hear it. This is an amazing young lady who's come to our town trying to find an end to all the heartache and grief she's been through. If not an end, at least a chance for a new start. I know folks are curious, and we've gotta tell them something. But I was hoping you could help me make sure that whatever we say helps folks understand how to treat her right, so Black Rock *can* be a new start for her, not just another place she needs to run away from."

CHAPTER 8

*B*y late afternoon, Theresa was completely spent. Fortunately, the house had already been cleaned by the maid service. Since that nice deputy left, she'd spent all her time unloading boxes. Most contained the new things she'd purchased in Asheville. She'd spent a couple of weeks there after Thanksgiving in a large, unfurnished apartment. Mainly, to give her a place to put all the things she was buying for the house in Black Rock. By the end of that shopping spree, there was barely any room left in the apartment to walk around.

After the plane crash, her place in Brooklyn was almost completely destroyed. Either by fire or the freezing water the firemen used to put the fire out. She'd only been able to salvage two small boxes of mostly personal things. For the next eighteen months, she'd lived with her family. Then out of the blue, a lawyer contacted her about a class-action lawsuit his firm was pursuing against the airlines, on behalf of families who'd lost loved ones in the crash. She agreed to become a part of the lawsuit, never imagining that a few months later she'd be handed a check for over three-hundred-thousand-dollars.

At the time, she had no savings account and a total of eighty-four dollars in her checkbook. The sum she'd received was incomprehensible. She had no reference point for how much money she now had, or the many things she could now afford. Every single item in the Brooklyn apartment was either a hand-me-down from family members or used things they'd bought at a thrift store. The concept of having extra cash at the end of the month was unthinkable. On the contrary, she and Tom sweated through the last week of every month hoping, somehow, they'd have enough money left to make rent. It was one of the reasons they were the only family in the building who didn't have a TV yet.

Tom would be completely flabbergasted to see her now, in this town, in this house, with all these new things. The odd thing was, even with all their worthless possessions and furnishings back in Brooklyn, they were happy. There had always been the hope that someday their situation would improve, though neither one knew how. It was fun just talking about the possibility of having nicer things, regardless of how far off in the future they seemed, or how long they'd have to wait to get them.

Here she was, now surrounded by more and even fancier things than either of them had ever imagined. But having them — without Tom or the kids here — couldn't even put a smile on her face, let alone produce any joy in her heart. They were just things. Nice things. But still, just things. As she emptied each box, she'd break it down flat and add it to a growing pile in the garage.

And with each visit to the garage, she'd marvel at the shiny new car occupying one side. It was a bright red Chevy

Nova. They had just started making them this year. Her father helped pick it out then had to teach her how to drive. Fortunately, it had an automatic transmission. But she was still terrified of it for the first few weeks.

Driving it now was actually fun, one of the few things these days that could generate a smile. Of course, she hadn't had to drive it in the snow yet. From what the realtor said, it almost always snowed in December in Black Rock. Maybe she could find someone local to give her some tips.

She came back in from the garage, decided to take a little break from unpacking. Walking over to the living room window, she glanced out at the scene. Except for a large front yard and a smaller backyard, her house was completely surrounded by thick evergreen trees. Supposedly, her actual property line in the back went about twenty-five yards beyond the tree line. Not much further beyond that, the ground sloped upward toward a big hill. The grass in the yard was mostly brown except for small clumps of snow lying about here and there from a snowfall that happened a few days before she arrived.

She walked over to her new console TV and turned it on. It was so much nicer than the TV set they had watched at the neighbors' apartment. This thing probably wouldn't even fit in their living room. It was like a fine piece of furniture. The TV was in the center with two built-in speakers on either side. When you lifted the wooden top, a stereo record player was on one side, and an AM/FM radio on the other. It cost about six hundred dollars. It was hard to fathom she had spent that much on something like a TV.

She turned the channel to CBS, which the salesman in Asheville said would likely be the station with the best reception in Black Rock. The other two networks could only be seen by houses on specific sides of the mountain. She'd forgotten which ones. But sure enough, CBS came right on. She backed up from the television and plopped down on the comfy sofa. Within minutes, she got sucked into a soap opera. She wasn't sure which one, until the commercial break where the announcer said: *"We'll be right back to The Secret Storm, after a word from our sponsors."*

Secret Storm...sounded intriguing. She hurried into the kitchen to refill her coffee, fixed it, then hurried back to the couch. Barely fifteen minutes had passed before the show was over. She must've come in halfway. After a few commercials, another one began called, *The Edge of Night.* The show had barely begun when she stood up, walked over to the TV, and turned it off. This was supposed to be a short break. If she wasn't careful, she'd sit there watching soap operas the rest of the afternoon. She had far too much work to do.

She got up and walked back to the stack of boxes she'd been unpacking. When she looked down and read the note written on one of them, her heart sank a little. It was one of the boxes of personal things she'd brought from the apartment.

Did she really have the strength to open it? Maybe she should just walk it over to the garage, unopened, and store it there. She picked it up and headed in that direction but stopped. She was being silly. She needed to look inside. If it was the one with Christmas things, it could be stored in the garage. Like the last two Christmases, she had no plans to decorate the house this season. There was just no point.

But the *other* box contained things like photo albums and other keepsakes she definitely did *not* want to store in the garage. She carried it over to the dining room table and opened the top flaps.

Immediately, she could tell...this was the Christmas box. Mostly ornaments for the tree, carefully wrapped in tissue paper. But sitting at the top was something that caused her heart to skip a beat. "Oh, my," she said aloud and released a sigh. She lifted it out and gazed at this beautiful little Christmas children's book, called *The Night before Christmas*.

On the cover, a big, chubby, rosy-cheeked Santa stood beside a fully decorated Christmas tree holding a brightly wrapped present. Involuntarily, familiar words began reciting in her mind — in Tom's voice—the first words of the famous poem by Clement Moore:

'TWAS THE NIGHT *before Christmas*
  When all through the house
  Not a creature was stirring,
  Not even a mouse...

"No," she yelled aloud and set the book back in the box. "I can't do this."

This was the kids' favorite Christmas book. It would be the only book they'd want read to them before bed every night, starting a week before Christmas until the last reading of the year on Christmas Eve. Of course, on that last time through, Tom would always read it with lots of extra drama, reminding the kids that "tonight's the night" when everything in this book happens, but only if they got "nestled in their beds" and went right to sleep.

She closed the lid and glanced at the door to the garage but decided not to store this box in there, afraid the extreme weather changes could damage the book. She remembered how huge her pantry was and decided to stick it in there, against the back wall...maybe behind something else so she wouldn't even see it.

She was glad the book had been spared the airplane crash but she wondered, would she really ever have a reason to look at this book again? Certainly not this Christmas, but really...would she ever want to celebrate Christmas again? She couldn't even imagine it.

CHAPTER 9

*T*he following morning, Bud had just finished pouring his coffee and walked back to his desk. Andy hadn't come in yet, but that wasn't surprising. He wasn't much of a stickler about getting to work on time. He'd never see it as being late. He'd usually leave the house on time, but Andy was quite the talker, saw it as one of his main duties to chat with the populace on his way in. Just keeping the peace he called it.

Bud didn't mind talking to folks if there was something worth hearing, or saying.

He had just sat down when the phone rang out in the reception area. Margie picked it up pretty quick. The door was closed, and normally Bud wouldn't hear anything Margie said. He was about to pick up the morning paper when her voice got louder. His ears perked up.

Suddenly, she burst through the door, glanced at Andy's empty desk, then looked over at Bud. "We got ourselves a problem, Deputy Wallace. I just got off the phone with Sarah

Wilmington. Someone broke into their house, stole quite a few things."

Bud sat up. "A robbery?"

"Sounds like it. She said they'd been gone a few days to a family funeral in Tennessee. Got back last night and could tell right off something was wrong. One of the kids noticed the dining room curtains moving. Sarah's husband turned on the light and they could all see, the curtains were moving because of the wind coming through a broken window."

Bud set his coffee down and stood. Didn't look like he was going to get to drink it hot today. "I'll get right on over there. They sure there's no one in the house? Everyone okay?"

"Everyone's fine," she said. "Her husband searched the whole house, figured the thief was long gone before they got home."

He grabbed his keys and jacket and headed for the door. "Let Andy know about this when he gets in."

TEN MINUTES LATER, Bud pulled up next to the curb outside the Wilmington's house. He'd been tempted to ride there with the lights flashing and sirens blaring. This was a bona fide crime. Hadn't had one of those in Black Rock for quite a spell. But he realized, that was an itch better left un-scratched. No sense drawing all that attention to himself and frightening all these folks along the way. Especially when the culprit — as the Wilmingtons said — was long gone.

Barely halfway up the sidewalk, Sarah came through the front door to meet him.

"Harold's working on the window, right now. We taped up some cardboard last night to keep the weather out. He's replacing that with wood until we can get a proper pane of glass in there."

Bud tried not to let his disappointment show. So much for not messing with the crime scene. Guess he could forget about dusting the window sill for fingerprints. They walked through the front door, felt nice to get warm again. "So, did the thief just break the one pane?"

She nodded. "Broke the one closest to the window latch. Must've unlocked it and slid it open enough to crawl in." She walked him back toward the dining room.

He could see her husband hard at work on the window project. "Morning, Harold."

He glanced Bud's way. "Morning, Bud. Wish I could visit with you, but I better get this done. Sarah knows everything that needs saying anyhow."

"That's all right. I'll just talk with her. But, you got any idea who might've done this? Any idea at all?"

He stopped, looked at Bud. "Been thinking about it off and on since I woke up. Can't think of nary a soul. Judging by what they took, they were looking for things they can sell. Not that anything we have is worth much."

"All right, thanks."

Sarah walked back to the living room. "I made a list of the things they took." She handed it to Bud. "As you'll see, he didn't get much worth selling, you ask me. Not like we have any fancy paintings or family jewels. He did get the family radio, but that thing was so old, not sure he could sell it for more than a couple bucks, if that." She looked over at Harold and said aloud for his benefit. "Maybe this'll get old stingy over there to finally buy his family a TV set. Think we're the only house on this block don't have one."

Bud looked over the list. "Did he ransack the place? Was it a mess when you got home and you cleaned it all up?"

"I wouldn't say ransacked," she said, "but he did make a good mess. Leaving drawers pulled out everywhere. In the bedrooms and in the kitchen. Did get a nice set of knives Harold bought me for Christmas last year. Wouldn't tell me what he paid for them, but I think they might be worth something."

"Okay with you if I dust some of those drawers for fingerprints?" Bud asked.

"If you think that'll help," she said. "Course, I'll never say no to someone dusting for me."

Bud laughed. "You might if you knew what I meant by the offer." He explained the process, the fine black powder involved. She got quite a look of concern. "But, I'll clean it right up once I check for prints. And thanks for this list. If we catch the culprit — and I'm sure we will — we can see if he has any of these things in his possession. He does, that'll help us convict him."

"Will we ever get any of the stuff back?"

"Sure, if we catch him, and he's still got any of it left." Bud walked into the kitchen. Thankfully, the drawers looked like they'd been untouched by the family. He took out his fingerprinting kit and set it on the counter.

First time he'd ever used it. Hope he remembered all the steps he'd learned from that class last year in Asheville.

CHAPTER 10

*A*fter finishing up at the Wilmington residence, Bud headed back to the office to brief Andy. When he walked in, Andy was eager to hear the update, his feet not resting on the desk, as usual when Andy drank his morning coffee.

"Sounds like I missed out on the excitement," Andy said. "The Wilmingtons okay?"

"A little shook up, but they're fine." Bud set some things down on his desk. "Talked to the neighbors before I left. Looks like the robber only broke into the one place."

"That's some relief," Andy said. "Whoever it was, probably knew they were out of town, which is why he picked their place instead of anyone else's."

"Thinking the same thing," Bud said. "And the fact he picked the empty place suggests he's not violent. Wasn't looking to hurt anyone, just get some free stuff."

"Hope you're right," Andy said. "How much you figure he stole?"

Bud held up the list. "Sarah made an inventory for us. My guess is, they'll only get a hundred dollars, or so, if they can sell it all. Maybe less."

"Hundred dollars isn't a whole lot, but it's not nothing. Especially for a kid."

"A kid?" Bud repeated. "You think our thief is a kid?"

"I don't mean a little kid," Andy said. "Thinking more like a teenager. I'd start asking any of those neighbors who have young-uns that age. Seems like it would have to be somebody who lived around them. How else would they know the Wilmingtons were out of town?"

"I'll do that," Bud said. "Figured I'd talk with Mr. Emerson, too."

"Pawnshop owner," Andy said. "Good thinking. Although, unless the kid is stupid — assuming it is a kid — he's not likely to sell the stuff in Black Rock. Not at the only pawnshop in town. Too easy to trace it back to him. I'd call all the pawnshops in nearby towns, too. Ask them to keep an eye out for someone trying to pawn any of the things on that list."

"Will do, Andy." Of course, Bud had already thought of these things, but he was glad to see he was on the right track.

AFTER BUNDLING UP, Theresa got into her new red Nova and drove into the downtown area of Black Rock. It felt almost exhilarating riding around all the curves and up and down the hills. All those years living in Brooklyn, she never knew how much fun it was to drive. Another contrast to life in Brooklyn was the traffic, or the absence of it. She only saw two cars on the road between her house and the store. And here in the store parking lot, maybe a dozen cars. That was all.

The grocery store itself, what a difference. It wasn't one of those big food stores like she'd seen in Asheville, but Philpott's Grocery was easily three times the size of the little corner stores in Brooklyn. And Philpott's was a standalone building. Even had grocery carts. She was glad, because she'd written quite a list. Her house had a nice big pantry just off the kitchen. She decided to fill up the shelves with enough dry goods to last the winter.

Of course, the freezer in her refrigerator wasn't that big, so she'd still have to regularly shop for the cold stuff, like dairy, meat, and vegetables. But she figured, since it was just her, she could get enough to last at least a week at a time. As she walked toward the carts, she overheard two women talking behind a station wagon. One was loading groceries into the car.

"Did you hear about what happened to Sarah?"

"I don't know. Heard Harold's uncle died last week, and they were attending his funeral."

"No, it's not that. They went to the funeral, but last night when they got home, they found out someone broke into their house while they were gone."

"Oh, no. That's terrible."

"Isn't it? The thief stole a bunch of things. Don't know exactly what. But apparently he broke in through a window in the back of the house."

Theresa moved away, so it wouldn't look like she was being nosy. She pulled out a cart and walked toward the doors. A squad car pulled into the parking lot. Bud was behind the wheel. He looked over at her, waved, and smiled. She smiled and waved back.

He drove over to her and stopped. Then leaned over the seat and rolled the window down halfway. "Hey, Theresa. How are you doing today?"

She left the cart on the sidewalk and stepped closer to his car. "Pretty good, I guess. Decided to take a break from all my unpacking and stock up on groceries."

"It's where I shop, too," he said. "If you wind up buying a lot, don't hesitate to ask the bag boy to help you load those groceries in your trunk. They do that for nothing at Philpott's."

"I'll try to remember that. Say..." She came closer. "Just heard two women talking about some family in town getting robbed last night. Someone named Sarah?"

"Yeah, afraid it's true. Here I was telling you how safe this town is, right? I was out there at the Wilmington's this morning checking out the scene. Just stopped in at the pawn-shop around the corner."

"In case the thief tries to sell what he stole there?"

"That's the idea. But hey, I don't think you have anything to worry about. This happened on the other side of town. Sheriff Andy and I are thinking it's probably some high-school kid who lives in the immediate area of the house that was broken into. Someone who would've known the Wilm-ingtons were out of town."

"The Wilmingtons?"

"That's Sarah's last name," he said. "It was their house that got robbed. Like I said, don't think you have anything to worry about. We'll get this guy, soon, I'm sure."

"I'm sure you will." She smiled and stepped back onto the sidewalk. "Well, guess I better get into the store. Nice to see you again."

"You too, Theresa. Take care." He rolled up the window and drove off.

She continued walking toward the front entrance, hoping Bud was right. After she got inside, she thought…just in case he wasn't, maybe she should look into buying herself a gun.

CHAPTER 11

*T*hree days later, and now less than a week from Christmas, Bud and Sheriff Andy were driving back to the south end of town after Margie took another frantic call from a resident about a break-in. Bud was driving. Andy read over the notes Margie had jotted down while the man spoke. The victim's name was Elmer Whitman, a widower in his sixties.

"It's gotta be the same guy," Andy said. "Elmer don't live but three blocks from the Wilmingtons. We haven't had a burglary in several years, and now we get two in the space of a week."

Bud turned off the main street and onto a street in Elmer's neighborhood. "Did I hear Margie say Elmer was home when the break-in occurred?"

"He was right upstairs sleeping," Andy said. "This thief — whoever he is — is getting bolder, I'll tell you that much."

"Guess the thief stayed downstairs," Bud said. "So, Elmer didn't hear a thing?"

"Slept right through it. Of course, old Elmer don't hear

too much more when he's awake. Guess you never talked with Elmer then?"

"Don't think I have," Bud said.

"Oh, you'd know if you had. You gotta almost yell for him to hear ya'." Andy read some more of Margie's note. "The culprit could've been making Jiffy Pop on the stove and Elmer wouldn't have heard him."

Bud laughed, picturing the scene. "It's Evergreen Drive, isn't it?"

"Yeah, the next street coming up. Elmer's place is about four or five houses down on the left." He glanced at the note again. "44 Evergreen. I told him we'd be right over. Of course, I said give us a few extra minutes since we're driving on snowy roads."

Bud turned right onto Elmer's street. "So far, it's not too bad. I'm guessing maybe three or four inches. Trickiest part is guessing where the road is underneath the snow." He was glad the roads were nearly empty.

"Supposed to be another foot falling closer to Christmas," Andy said. "Might have ourselves a genuine white Christmas this year, like Bing sings about in that song."

"Your kids'll love that," Bud said.

"I will, too. Folks can't get into too much mischief when they're snowed in. There's his place up on the left."

Bud saw the street number on the mailbox. "Quite a good-sized house for one man." He pulled over and they both got out. It was plenty cold, but at least the wind had died down compared to what it had been when Bud came in to work. He waited for Andy to walk around the car, so they could go in together. He felt pretty confident about handling this on his own, but Andy wanted to come along, so Bud would let him lead.

"Here's how I thought we'd play this," Andy said. "I'll do all the talking with Elmer, since I'm used to dealing with him. Just ignore all the yelling when it starts. He's supposed to have made up a list of what's missing, like Sarah did for us. You dust for fingerprints and make some good notes about the scene. Hopefully, those prints will match the ones you got at the Wilmington's."

Bud thought about something Andy said. "You know, Andy. The big city police in Mount Pilot use cameras now for crime scenes. Work way better than handwritten notes."

"Mount Pilot," Andy repeated, shaking his head. He caught the reference to the TV show and the fictitious "big city" near Mayberry that Andy and Barney were always referring to. "Guess I'll have to think about that, getting a camera. Maybe Santa will bring us one for Christmas. Come on, let's get up to the house."

Andy startled Bud by how loudly he banged on the front door. "Gotta do it. Only way he'll hear me." He waited a few long seconds then banged again.

"I'm coming, I'm coming. Hold your horses."

The door opened, and the two men quickly stepped inside.

They found Elmer all bundled up. It was just marginally warmer in the house than outside.

"Elmer, don't you have any heat in this place?" Andy yelled.

"I do. I got the thermostat turned up pretty good, though, so it don't come on very often. Trying to use up some of this firewood in the fireplace. If you want to talk over there, it's pretty warm."

"Yeah, let's do that. You got that list Margie told you about, right?"

"The one about all the things he stole? Got it right here." He pulled a sheet out of his overcoat pocket.

"While we talk, Deputy Wallace here will start checking things over, see what kind of evidence we can find. You know there was a break-in a couple days ago just a few blocks from here?"

"Sure did," Elmer said. "The whole neighborhood was talking about it. I figured I'd be safe because I don't ever go nowhere. Weren't the Wilmingtons out-of-town?"

"Yes," Andy yelled. "That concerns me."

As they continued talking, Bud began exploring the downstairs. Like the first robbery, the place was a mess. All the drawers in every room were pulled out. This time, the thief didn't break through a dining room window. He broke a pane of glass on the kitchen door, the one closest to the knob. Bud brought his fingerprint kit over and set it on the nearest counter.

There weren't any prints on the door. Bud realized, it was probably snowing when he broke in, so the thief likely wore gloves. But maybe he took them off as he tried opening some of the kitchen counter drawers. A few minutes later... Bingo! Got some really good ones on the silverware drawer.

He did a few more drawers in the kitchen, then a couple more in the dining room. Figured that was enough. All the while, he could hear Andy yelling answers back to Elmer in the other room. After putting his kit away and cleaning up the mess, Bud decided to do Elmer a favor. Maybe he could find a piece of cardboard he could tape over the opening in the broken window, to keep the cold from blowing in.

He zipped up his coat and made his way out the kitchen door toward the freestanding garage. He didn't get very far before noticing a row of footprints tracking both to and away from the kitchen door. They weren't perfect but clear enough for Bud to tell they ran along the side of the house and down the driveway. He imagined last night this whole area was covered in shadows.

As he squatted down to examine one of the better set of footprints, he made an observation. Or as Sherlock Holmes would call it, a deduction. The thief must've broken in after the snow had already begun, then left before the snow finished falling. If he'd come before the snow, his prints would have been completely covered. If he came after, they'd have been perfectly preserved. Bud could see the outline of the prints but also that at least an inch of snow had filled in the indentation made by the man's shoes, or boots.

He stood back up but kept his eyes focused on the footprints. Man, did he wish he had a camera. Then he got an idea. He picked one of the clearer footprints and stepped his own foot into the snow beside it. Bud's imprint was just slightly bigger. He wore a size 10. Maybe this guy wore a size 9. Of course, Bud was thinking boot size, not shoe size.

But who would go out into a snowstorm without boots?

After getting some cardboard for the window, he went back inside and made some notes. After covering the window he decided, the heck with this. He had a perfectly good camera at home. He'd clear it with Andy first, but he was thinking he should go home and bring back a ruler and a camera, get some shots of these footprints before it snowed anymore. As Andy said, sometime between now and Christmas they were supposed to get another foot.

MEANWHILE, on the north end of town, Theresa peered out her front window, mesmerized by the scene. She had never seen anything quite so beautiful, at least in person. And unlike the snow that occasionally would fall in Brooklyn, the scene here would stay just as lovely for many hours, if not days. There weren't any dirty cars, trolleys, or buses to plow through it and turn this winter wonderland into horrible brown slush.

It made her think of that line from one of her favorite Johnny Mathis Christmas songs: *It'll nearly be like a picture print by Currier and Ives.* That album — like the rest of their record collection — had been destroyed by the crash. It almost made her want to go out and buy it again once the roads were cleared.

Almost.

CHAPTER 12

A few hours later, Theresa thought she heard the rumbling of a car outside, so it was close by. She was in the pantry which shared a wall with the garage. She wouldn't have heard a car driving by on the street. She hadn't planned to be in the pantry but got distracted after storing the Christmas box in here. After buying so many groceries, especially dry goods, she never got a chance to get things organized.

She hurried into the living room to look out the window. It had the best view of the driveway. It was that Sheriff deputy's car, Bud. She was almost happy to see him. He'd been so nice to her so far and didn't seem to have any ulterior motives for doing so. On the other hand, his car had just messed up the beautiful Christmas scene outside. Two evenly-spaced tire marks had torn through the pristine white landscape. Coming down the hill on the left then turning into the street in front of her house, and finally down her driveway.

Oh well, it was still way better than what she'd have seen back home in Brooklyn.

She watched as Bud, all bundled up, got out of the car and made his way through the snow toward the front door. As he stepped onto the porch, she opened the door. "Come on in, so I can close the door. It's freezing out there."

He banged his boots on the porch floor. "Don't want me dragging all this snow in the house, do ya?"

"No, guess not. Just hurry." She tried to sound playful, hoped it didn't come off as bossy. When he made it inside, she closed the door behind him. "What are you doing driving out in this crazy weather?"

He gave her a look, then grinned. "Theresa, this isn't crazy. It's just a few inches, maybe five or six in some places. Is this much snow considered a crazy amount in Brooklyn?"

"Maybe, I don't know. Maybe it's just me. In Brooklyn when it snows, in no time at all — between all the traffic and the plows — the roads are all clear. The snow gets piled up in clumps. Big ugly clumps."

"That sounds pretty horrible."

"Ever seen any Christmas cards with winter scenes of Brooklyn on them?"

He laughed. "Can't say I have."

"Well, I've seen plenty with scenes like I was just seeing out my window...before you drove your car through it, that is." She started leading him out of the foyer into the living room.

"Sorry about that. But in a couple of days, you'll have that pretty scene back. Supposed to be a real snowstorm coming. I guarantee you won't even see my car tracks after that. And that'll almost guarantee a white Christmas here in Black Rock."

She forced a smile. "That'll be nice. Want some coffee? Probably still fresh. Could make you some tea or hot chocolate?"

"I'd love some, but I really can't stay. Thought I'd drive over here and give you some news before you heard it on the grapevine."

"You drove all the way out here — in *this*?" Pointing to the weather outside. "— to tell me some news?"

"Theresa, I'm telling ya', this weather is nothing. Not for a local like me. Now after that snowstorm in a couple days…"

"Okay," she said. "I guess, it's just…for me, I'd be terrified. I've never driven in snow."

"Well, I can imagine that could be a scary thing. Especially with these roads, being so hilly and winding. If you'd like, I could show you how. Give you some tips, some things to avoid. Stuff like that."

"Really? I would love that."

"I couldn't do it now. I'm still on duty. But I get off at five. I could come back then, take you for a drive. It shouldn't take too long."

"Okay, if you're sure you don't mind. Don't know if I'll be doing anymore driving before that snowstorm comes. But it would be nice to know how to drive in snow like, like this. You know, a few inches or so."

"Then we'll plan on it. I could give you a call if something came up, and I couldn't make it. You have a phone yet?"

She walked over to an end table, pointed down. "Had them installed yesterday. Got another one in the kitchen on the wall, and another next to my bed." She started walking toward the kitchen. "Got a pad next to the kitchen phone. Let me write my number down."

A few moments later, she handed him the piece of paper.

"This just gave me a thought. Not that I'll ever need the police in a town like this, but if I did, who would I call? I mean, I wrote down the Sheriff's office number, but you said you get off at five. What if I had a need to reach you guys after five?"

"Well, like you said, a town like Black Rock, we haven't needed to have a nighttime shift, guess you could call it. Just not enough stuff happens. But folks know they can still call that number. Phone company set things up so that it rings at Margie's house when the office is closed. She takes the call and decides if it's serious enough to bother Andy. If so, she'll call him. Guess she should really just call me. The few times it's happened, he's called me to go handle it. It never amounted to much."

"So, just call the same number then?" she said. "For the Sheriff's office?"

He nodded. "But hey, show me that pad. I'll write my number down. Since they'd probably wind up calling me anyway, might as well skip the steps in between."

"Sure, if you don't mind. Follow me." She walked back to the kitchen, showed him the pad attached to a board hanging on the wall beside the phone. He wrote his number down right under the number for the Sheriff's office. They walked back into the living room.

"So, what was the news you drove out here to tell me?"

Bud made a face, like the question surprised him.

"What's the matter?"

"It's nothing. It's just…here I was, going on and on about how safe the town is, and the reason I came out here was to let you know we had another break-in last night."

"Oh, no."

"Afraid so. But really, Theresa, like the last one, it's really nothing to worry about. We're 95% sure it's the same guy. Happened just a few blocks away from the last one. And both of those are way on the other side of town."

"Way on the other side? Bud, you and I both know it only takes about five minutes to drive from one side of Black Rock to the other."

"Okay, that's true. But Andy and I are thinking this is probably somebody that lives in that neighborhood. And he hasn't hurt anybody. The folks who got robbed didn't even know it happened until long after the thief was gone. Just seems like someone bent on stealing things he can sell."

Theresa looked all around the living room and dining area. "You mean like all this new stuff I just bought for this house?"

Bud laughed. "I see your point. But seriously, Theresa, I don't think whoever it was will wind up over here on Elk Hill Road."

"Well, I'm glad to hear you say that. But you are, unlike me, a big strong guy who carries a gun. Not sure you can totally relate to my situation. Which is why…I went to the gun store in town and bought me a pistol."

"That's okay. I mean, it's a free country and anyone can own a gun. But seriously, you really are safe here."

"I probably am. But all the same, if not for robbers then maybe for wild animals. I live right here on the edge of the woods."

"Well, yeah, for that…it kinda makes sense, you owning a gun. You know how to use it? Safely, I mean. Ever had any lessons?"

"No. Never fired a gun in my life. You think maybe when you come back to teach me how to drive in the snow, you could show me what to do?"

"Well, yeah, I could do that. Might be too dark after our driving lesson in the snow. Might have to come back to show you how to handle that gun. And it's not just the shooting part, you need to know how to clean it, too. Keeping it clean is very important."

"Okay, guess the gun lesson will have to wait. Probably till after that snowstorm, if it's coming in a couple of days."

"Probably will," Bud said, "have to wait I mean. But there's no hurry. I guarantee, you won't need to know how to use that gun till then."

CHAPTER 13

The day was wearing long. Ransom had no way of knowing how many miles they had traveled since burying their Pa and saying goodbye to their cabin for the last time. The only home they'd ever known. But he knew this had been the fourth day of their journey. And he knew, from what Pa had said before he died, there were three days left until Christmas.

It was plenty cold out, especially at night. They were kept a little warmer by wearing their parents' big coats. Pa had insisted Ransom take them when they left. It was a hard thing to do, but he knew it had to be done. Emma cried about it a good bit, thinking Pa would be so cold in that ground without his coat on. It gave Ransom a chance to explain to her about heaven. Not that he knew that awful much. But he did know his folks were in a much better place. A place where they never got too hot, or too cold. Where the weather was never bad. And folks never got sick no more.

And the best part…no one ever died.

Ransom learned all this from his Ma before she died. And

his Pa reminded him of the same the day before he passed. When Emma wasn't too close, he whispered to Ransom to keep talking about heaven with his sister after he was gone. It would help her from getting overcome with sorrow.

"How much longer do we have to travel, Ransom?"

He stopped dragging the pull-sleigh he'd made and turned to face her. That's the main reason the going was so slow. He had to drag her through the woods on that sleigh, along with all the stuff he could fit on it from home. "Not too much longer, Emma."

"I'm getting tired. And it seems like the sun's going down."

"It's gone down some. But it's also getting a little cloudy. Kinda makes it seem darker than it is. I figure we got maybe an hour or two left before I'll have to stop. Give me time to collect enough firewood to last the night."

"Could we make it just one hour, not two?"

Ransom laughed, wondering if Emma had any idea how much more tired a body gets dragging this here sleigh, versus sitting on it. "All right. I'll try to keep it to an hour." He started pulling again. At least now, and for the whole day so far, they were going slightly downhill.

After a couple minutes, Emma said, "If it's getting cloudy, how do you know which way to go in these woods? Everything looks the same to me."

She'd asked a similar question the first day, when it was totally sunny. He'd explained to her what Pa had said about the sun always rising in the east and setting in the west. He could figure out where south was from that. Now he explained something else Pa had taught him. "Well for one thing, before it got cloudy, I was able to get oriented about which way we needed to go. But now I can pay attention to the moss growing on the trees." He stopped and pointed to one. "See what I mean? You can see it on lots of 'em. Moss likes to grow on the north side. So, I just head in the opposite direction. The trees help another way. The branches like to grow on the south side, since they get sun for the longest part of the day. So, I look at which side's got more branches. Between those two things, how can I go wrong?"

"Think I'll ever be as smart as you?" she said.

"Sure. you will, Emma. Someday you might even be way smarter, once we both start going to school. That's one of the main reasons Pa told me we had to leave the cabin. So, we could get book learning. I especially can't wait till I can read."

"You're plenty smart now," she said. "You learn to read, I'll never catch up."

"Naw. Everything I just told you about knowin' where to go came from Pa."

That seemed to settle her curiosity down. No one spoke for the next few minutes. But then, sadly, Ransom heard a sound he'd quickly come to recognize these past few days. He looked back at Emma. She was crying. And he knew why. "It was cause I talked about Pa, wasn't it?" She nodded. It was almost hard to see, her being wrapped so tightly in Ma's big coat. He got down and scrunched in beside her, put his arm around her shoulder. "It's okay to cry, Emma. I know you miss him. We both do."

"But I don't see you ever crying."

"Oh, I been crying plenty. Off-and-on since we started. I just don't ever turn around and let you see. What good would it do for you to see that? It'd just start you crying, too. Then I'd feel bad about missing Pa, and about making you sad."

She thought on that. "You *sure* he's in heaven with Ma?"

"I'm sure, Emma."

73

"Tell me again how you know."

"When Ma knowed she was dying, she used to read to me from the Bible. All about how faith in Jesus is the reason we can know where we'll end up. We're supposed to be good as we can be down here, but it's not why God lets us in. It's on account of Jesus, and us trusting him and what he did on the cross that makes all the difference. Pa believed that. He believed in Jesus. Prayed to him every day. So, don't you worry. They're together again. I'm sure of it."

He looked down at her. Her crying stopped. "Think we can get a move on it again?"

She nodded.

He got up and started pulling that sleigh some more, wondering himself how much farther he could go before his strength gave out.

CHAPTER 14

*B*ased on something he saw up ahead, Ransom could hardly believe their luck. Then he remembered how Ma once said there weren't no such thing as luck. What folks should be doing when they think they got lucky was thank God instead for his kindness. So, that's what he did. First on his own, like a prayer. Then to Emma. "Say, Emma, you see that up ahead, that dark place through those trees?"

She bent over to the right, so she could see around him. "I do. What is it?"

Emma hated the dark. He better think of something quick, so she'd see it as a good thing. "Pretty sure it's a cave. God has answered your prayers. If it is, we can stop there for the night."

"I'm not sure I was praying," she said. "More like just hoping. Seems like it's been getting colder the farther we go, and my bottom is awful sore."

Ransom picked up his pace. Now that he had a destination, he got a second wind. But he had to be careful. The hill they'd been walking down seemed a little steeper than before. And there were so many trees to navigate around.

In just a few minutes, they were there. And it was a cave. With a good-sized opening. Carved into a section of hillside running back up in a different direction.

"Ransom, it's so dark in there."

"I know, Emma. But it won't be after I build a fire. First things first, gotta go make sure the cave's empty." He took his rifle in both hands. "You wait here. I'll go check."

"You're leaving me? By myself?"

"I gotta, Emma. There's no other way. But you'll be all right. Won't be gone but a minute." He turned around and bent down, said a quick prayer over her, like Ma always prayed whenever they left the cabin. Prayed for protection and for angels to watch over 'em. "I'll be right back. I promise." Slowly, he headed into the mouth of the cave, wishing badly he had a lantern or some kind of torch. About five feet in, he grabbed a small stone and tossed it as far as he could. He couldn't see where it went, but he could hear it bouncing off the rocks until it stopped.

Then he listened.

"Thank you, Lord," he said aloud. Total silence. No animals growling or coming his way.

Just to be sure, he threw another one. Same thing happened, which made him feel pretty sure the cave was really empty. He didn't have the courage to go in much farther, not as dark as it was. He headed back out to tell Emma. "It's safe, Emma. We'll stay here tonight."

"You mean, I can get up?"

"More than that, why don't you help me gather some firewood? Just grab all the little pieces you can and put 'em in a pile. I'll go round up some bigger pieces."

"But you won't go far?"

"No," he said. "No need to. Look at all the wood lying around. You'll be able to see me the whole time." He put the rifle around his shoulder and started gathering up some wood. As he did, he kept glancing back at Emma to make sure she was okay. She was. In fact, had a big smile on her face as she made her little pile of sticks.

TWENTY MINUTES LATER, Ransom was just about to light the firewood when he noticed a distinct smell in the air. He sniffed in deeply. "Emma, you smell that?"

"Smells like someone else's got a fire going," she said.

"Sure does." He stood up, checked the wind with his finger. Blowing slightly toward them from the south.

"What could it mean, Ransom?"

He looked down at her smiling. "Think it means we're not too far from some other folks. Maybe even city folks are nearby. Pa told me some of them have houses so big, two or three cabins like ours would fit inside. They got big fire-places in them, too. And electricity."

"What's that?"

"Not exactly sure how it works. But Pa said it does all kind of things we can never imagine. Lights turn on without lanterns or candles. And the whole house gets warm, not just by the fireplace."

Her face lit up as she tried to conjure up the scene. "Why don't we keep going instead of stopping at this cave? Maybe another hour or so we'll find one of them places."

"Little while ago you were wanting to stop in the worst way. Your bottom don't hurt no more?"

"It's a little sore but feels better since I got up and gathered all this wood."

"No, I don't think we should go any farther. Not tonight. I need to get this fire going, so we don't freeze. Besides, just smelling that smoke in the air...no telling how far it traveled on the wind. Could be miles away."

"Okay, if you say so. But maybe tomorrow? Think we might get to the city tomorrow?"

"I think so," he said. "But I need to stop talking and get working on this fire."

Two hours later, Ransom and Emma were resting comfortably *inside* the cave with a nice fire going and both their bellies full. In fact, Emma had already drifted off to sleep. Ransom could hardly believe how nice this cave turned out to be.

After he had made the first fire, the one *outside* in front of the cave, he'd taken one of the branches that had a nice fire going on the end of it, and used it to explore the cave a little. The first thing he discovered was, after going back about ten feet, it curved to the right and opened to an area almost the size of the big room in their cabin. That's as far into the hill as the cave went. But standing there he noticed the second thing. The smoke from his torch wasn't filling up the room like he expected. He figured he only had a matter of seconds before he'd start coughing and choking and have to hurry outside.

But that didn't happen.

Instead, the smoke went up toward the roof of the cave and disappeared into some kind of hole. Whatever it was, it must've gone all the way to the outside. So with Emma's help, and using his torch, he relocated their fire and their stuff inside the cave instead of out front. This was actually kinda nice.

He was pretty tired himself but decided to take advantage of Emma being sound asleep and — after grabbing the rifle — headed outside a few minutes. He was just curious about that smoke they'd smelled a little while ago. Wondered if he could still smell it.

Sure enough, he could. In fact, if anything it was even stronger. Coming from the same direction. Made him wonder if there were more than one fireplace in play. The hill they came down to get to this cave continued on down a ways farther. He hadn't brought a lit-stick from the fire with him, so he didn't want to venture out too far. But some of the moonlight was breaking through the trees, so he decided to venture just a little ways down the hill.

After maybe thirty or forty yards, he saw something that stopped him dead in his tracks. At first, he thought maybe it was the eyes of a wild animal in the distance, the way they glow sometimes when light hits 'em just right. Then he realized, couldn't be that. The light he saw shining through the trees was too bright to come from any animal, and not the right shape neither.

He squatted down and stared at it for a few minutes, trying to make sense of it. The only thing he could figure was, maybe the lights were coming from some cabin way off in the distance beyond the woods.

Or maybe, he thought, maybe the lights were coming from one of them big houses Pa had talked about.

Wouldn't that be something?

CHAPTER 15

Theresa was actually enjoying this, making spaghetti and meatballs for somebody.

As promised, Bud had come over after he got off work to show her how to drive in the snow. They had driven on Elk Hill Road the whole time and didn't actually see anyone else the entire hour. That suited her just fine.

Bud was a good teacher, way more patient than her father had been last year when he taught her how to drive. If Bud ever got tense, he didn't let it show. At first, he did the driving, explaining things as he did them. Then he pulled over and had her drive until she felt confident doing everything he'd said. By the time she pulled into the driveway, it was totally dark out except for the light from a half-moon that moved in and out between clouds.

She'd thanked him profusely, insisting he had probably saved her life. He'd laughed and said he was happy to do it. She could tell he meant it. When Bud headed toward his car, she just blurted out, "How about I make you some spaghetti and meatballs? You know, to thank you properly."

He instantly agreed, saying it was one of his favorite things to eat, but they didn't have any Italian restaurants in Black Rock. She'd asked him how did he ever get to eat it then and was horrified when he replied: "*Chef Boyardee.*"

For the last fifteen minutes, Bud sat on a nearby stool while she cooked. And they talked. It was nice. He was almost as easy to talk to as Tom had been. Of course, they didn't look or sound anything alike.

"I never knew how much went into making spaghetti and meatballs," he said. "All those cans of sauce and spices. And the meatballs, I've never seen them made by hand."

Theresa's family recipe called for using tomato sauce, tomato paste, crushed tomatoes, and fresh garlic. She gave it a good stir and said, "It may look like a lot of work, but I could do this in my sleep. Must've made it a hundred times. Of course, you're not gonna get the full flavor of how it tastes when I usually make it. After putting the sauce together, I usually let it simmer for hours." She gave it a sniff. "But I'm a hundred percent sure it will taste way better than Chef Boyardee. A thousand percent better."

"Those meatballs smell delicious."

She looked over at him. "They taste even better than they smell."

"How did you learn to cook such good Italian food? Dempsey sounds Irish."

"Yeah, my Tom was Irish. But that's my married name. When he met me, I was Theresa Sardelli. I grew up making this stuff. And all kinds of other Italian dishes. Lasagna, baked ziti, manicotti, and minestrone...that's a soup. Tom had never tasted any of them. But he wound up loving every one. Think the only Irish thing I made was corned beef and cabbage."

"One of our diners serves that on St. Patty's day," Bud said.

No one said anything a few moments as she finished up the meatballs. She had a feeling he was focused on her. But when she looked at him, he was actually looking all around the downstairs, at least as much as he could see from his stool. She stole the moment to look at him a little more closely than she'd ever dared, if he was looking at her. He was quite a handsome guy. And she especially loved how safe she felt being around him. As far as she could tell, he hadn't attempted to hit on her, not even once. She was so used to guys doing that, really since she turned thirteen. Her Tom was one of the first guys she'd met who didn't treat her that way. She was pretty sure that's what first attracted her to him. If anything, Tom had played hard to get. By the time he'd finally started looking at her *that way*, she was nuts about him.

Bud looked at her. She quickly looked at the meatballs.

"Theresa, mind if I ask...why did you buy such a big house?"

"I don't mind you asking. It was the only house for sale in Black Rock. I didn't really want a house this big, but I really wanted to move here. And I had the money, so I decided not to wait for something smaller to become available." She took a few minutes to explain to him about all the money she'd gotten from the lawsuit. She didn't know why exactly, but she had no problem telling him things like this.

After draining the grease off the meatballs, she gently poured them into the spaghetti sauce. "We're getting close now, Bud." He smiled, looked as if he wanted to ask something else but wasn't sure he should. "Better check on the pasta. Is there...something else on your mind?"

"I don't want to pry," he said.

"You let me be the judge. Go ahead and ask. If it's something I'm not okay to talk about, I'll tell you."

He nodded. "Okay, well, I'm noticing your house has no Christmas decorations up, and it's only a few days from now. I know that tragedy you went through two years ago happened close to Christmas. Has that kind of soured you on celebrating Christmas anymore?"

She stopped stirring the meatballs in the sauce and sighed. How much should she say?

"Really, you don't have to answer that. It's none of my business."

"No, it's a fair question. If we're going to be friends, I should be able to answer that."

"I can understand why you'd struggle with it. Well, listen to me...as if I could even begin to understand what you've been through. I just mean—"

"You don't have to apologize. I certainly do hope one day I'll be able to celebrate Christmas again. Until the crash, it was my favorite time of year. Nothing else even came close. Tom and the kids? Well, they made it so special. Now it just seems...I don't know, empty. Like I don't have any reason to do all the things I used to do. I guess for me, it was about sharing it all with them. And obviously, instead of being one of the best times of the year, now it's just...the time of year when God took away my family."

"I'm sorry, Theresa. I shouldn't have brought this up."

"That's okay, Bud. For some reason, it almost feels a little better talking about it. I really don't want to stay this way. I've prayed about it, quite a lot. I mean, one of the main reasons I moved here was to get a fresh start. Everything back in Brooklyn just reminded me of what I'd lost, not just at Christmas time. I'm hoping here, I can at least someday feel good about Christmas again." The spaghetti noodles were done. She turned off the burner.

"I just don't think this year's gonna be that year."

"I get that, Theresa. And for what it's worth, I think you got the right outlook. I'm certainly no expert on stuff like this, but I don't think this is something God expects you to fix. I don't know what the fix is, but it seems very much like a God thing."

"Nothing's impossible with God, right?" She pointed to a plaque hanging above the stove, which said the same thing. "My mom gave me that last Christmas. And in her own way, said something similar to what you just said. Of course, last year wasn't the year it got fixed, either." Theresa poured the pasta into the strainer.

"Who knows, maybe next year will be."

CHAPTER 16

The next morning, Ransom woke up and looked around. At first, he wasn't totally sure if he was still dreaming. Nothing looked familiar. The room was mostly dark, but there was some light coming in to the right. He sat up and looked around, then his eyes began to adjust. Now, he remembered.

They were in a cave.

He glanced over at Emma. She was still asleep. Looking back at the opening and judging by the brightness of the light coming in, the morning was well underway. He stood, stretched, and rubbed his eyes. The fire had completely gone out. That was probably the first thing he needed to fix. He picked up the rifle and made his way to the cave opening. Stepping outside, he slowly surveyed the scene. He didn't see or hear any animals, except for a collection of songbirds going at it in the trees.

One glance upward confirmed what he'd thought. They had slept in. Judging by where the sun hung in the sky, it was probably after 10 o'clock. He looked back at the cave, wondering if he should wake Emma up. Then he decided against it, realizing there was plenty of firewood scattered throughout the woods nearby. He'd just make sure the mouth of the cave was always in view.

Twenty minutes later, he had gathered enough wood to last at least till midafternoon. While he was building the fire, Emma awoke.

"Where are we?"

"In a cave. Remember last night?"

"Oh, yeah. Not used to it being dark when I wake up. You know, since we started our trip."

"It'll be plenty bright in a few minutes, once I get this fire going. If you want to see something real bright, go outside. Sun's already high in the sky."

"What time is it?"

"Not sure. Think it's after ten anyway. You hungry? I know I am."

Now she seemed fully awake. "I am. But I'm not really looking forward to breakfast. I checked the basket last night. All we got left is some of that last batch of jerky Pa made. My tummy doesn't want that."

"Yeah, that doesn't sound like anything I want for break-fast either. Everything else is gone?"

She nodded yes. "Can you go hunt us some food? Not that I'm really in the mood for meat, but we'll need some for later."

"Afraid I can't, Em. I didn't tell you last night, because you fell asleep so fast. But I went down that hill aways in the direction of that smoke we were smelling."

"You left me in here by myself?"

"I didn't go far. Didn't have to. Just down the hill I could see lights through the trees. Couldn't make out any details, but there's definitely somebody making those lights."

"Really? Why don't we just go there now? Maybe they got bacon and eggs?"

Ransom smiled. "Sorry to disappoint you, but I don't think that's a good idea. That, nor the hunting."

"Why?"

"You remember what Pa said about the law?"

"Some of it."

"Well, I remember all of it. He made me repeat it over and over. They're the folks in charge. They wear uniforms and guns. Pa said they're mostly good, only arresting people who do bad things."

"What's arresting?"

"It means they put people in jail. Lock them up in a cage."

"I don't want to be put in a cage."

"Well, that's what they do with bad people. Probably not what they'd do to us. But Pa said we don't want to get caught by them, because they might split us up. You go one way, and I go another, and we don't see each other anymore."

Emma started to cry.

"I won't let that happen. I promise. But that's why I can't hunt for food. Not anymore. I shoot that rifle at some critter and folks in the house beyond those trees will hear it. They might call the law, and we can't have that."

"So, what are we gonna do for food?"

"Well, for now, guess we gotta eat that jerky in the basket. In a little while, we'll head down that hill in the direction where I saw those lights. See what we can see from the trees. Hopefully, we'll see something good."

"You mean like some church folk?"

He smiled. "Yeah, Emma. Some nice church folk."

She got on her knees, headed for the food basket, then stopped and turned around. "Ransom, what are church folk?"

He smiled. What could he say? He wasn't all that sure himself.

LESS THAN AN HOUR LATER, Ransom and Emma were making their way down the hill toward the spot he'd seen the lights last night. He left the sled and most of their stuff in the cave. He told her he wanted to check out the situation first, make sure they'd be okay. The ground was pretty hard but not slippery. There were still clumps of snow gathered around the trees and resting in many of the branches, but there were plenty of places to walk in between the trees.

Ransom had brought the rifle just in case. But really, he hadn't seen any animals in the last twenty-four hours, and he couldn't find any animal prints in the area around the cave. Still, better safe than sorry.

After a few minutes more, the ground began to level out like they were at the bottom of the hill. Suddenly, through the trees up ahead Ransom saw something. At first, he wasn't sure what it was. A building of some kind, but definitely not a cabin. Whatever it was, it was huge.

"Quick, Emma, get down. Stay behind me."

"What is it, Ransom?"

"I'm not sure. We ain't ever seen a city. Pa told me they had all kinds of different buildings, like ones we'd never seen. Maybe that's what this is. Can you see up ahead between those trees?"

With most of her body still tucked behind him, she peered out around his shoulder. "I do see something. Looks like the trees end, then there's a clearing. Then...then I don't know what. What is it?"

"Pa said they call their cabins houses. Must be a house, but I never imagined it'd be so big."

"You see any people?" she said. "Any...church folk?"

"No. Let's get closer. But stay behind me, like you're doing."

They kept moving forward until they got to within a few feet of the clearing. Now they could see the building plain as day. Ransom didn't know what he imagined he'd find when they got to the city, but he hadn't imagined this. If this was a house, were they all this big?

"What are we gonna do now?" Emma said.

Ransom wasn't at all sure. One thing he did know, he wasn't ready to leave these woods until he could be sure it was a safe thing to do. "I think we should go back to the cave till it gets dark. I don't see any people, church folk or otherwise. I'll come back here when it's dark, when I can check this place out without being seen."

"So, no bacon and eggs?" Emma said.

"Sorry, Em. It's just not safe yet."

CHAPTER 17

*I*t had been a long, boring day for Ransom. Really, he had nothing to do.

Before lunchtime, got enough firewood collected to last three days. After that, what else was there? Couldn't hunt. Had no chores. And as for lunchtime, well, weren't hardly nothing to eat. Least Emma had her doll to play with, and to give her doll some company, Ransom cobbled together some sticks to look like a little man. Made him about the same size, told Emma she could pretend he was the doll's brother.

Thing was, she couldn't have been happier. She was at that age where she could just make up stuff in her head, and it would be so. Ransom had no idea what she saw when she looked at his little stick creation, but he looked way better to her than the thing he'd made. He remembered when he used to be able to play like that. Seemed like a long time ago, but when he thought on it, he realized it was just last year. Pa getting so sick and staying sick for so long, pretty much stole all his time to play. And if he ever got a sliver of time for himself, he had no interest in playing that way anymore. The kind of play where you make up stuff in your head.

But that gave Ransom an idea. And that idea helped him pass the time along.

If he figured it right, tomorrow was Christmas Eve. Sadly, leaving the cabin like they did, he had no time to think about presents. Pa was certainly way too sick to make any, like he did most years. Ransom did bring the collection of soldiers Pa had carved for him the last several Christmases. Had them in his special box. Every year Pa would make three or four more. They looked just like real men, only a couple inches tall. Half wore blue painted uniforms, and the other half gray.

Pa told him all about this big war that happened a hundred years ago between people in the north, and those who lived where they lived, in the South. Told him all kinds of tales of these different battles where thousands of soldiers fought, often to the death. Of course, Ransom being at that age like Emma, when he played with Pa's soldiers, that's what he'd see going on in front of him. Not a smattering of fifteen or twenty little soldiers, but hundreds going at it. He could hear the men yelling, the rifles firing off, even cannons exploding all around.

Ransom couldn't see such things anymore. He saw what everybody else saw. Little wooden soldiers piled together in a box. Though he didn't play with them now, he'd never be rid of them. They were his fondest treasures.

So, that's how Ransom spent the rest of his day. Trying to do for Emma what Pa had done for him all those Christmases before he got sick. He'd worked on carving up a really nice-looking brother for Emma's doll, one that looked a tad closer to a little boy than just a pile of sticks tied together.

By day's end, he'd made decent progress. Though it was a far cry from what Pa could've done. But at least he'd have something to give Emma come Christmas morning.

NIGHT HAD FINALLY COME, and Emma had finally fallen asleep.

When they ate the last of their food at dinnertime, Ransom had explained to her what he planned to do. Part of it anyways. She hated the idea and begged him to let her come along. But that would never work, not with what he had in mind. But he couldn't tell her that, so he said the kind of things Pa used to tell him if he ever had to leave them in the cabin after dark. "It's too dangerous, you have to stay here." And then the other one, "Trust me, you're gonna be fine."

Of course, Emma quickly pointed out that Pa had never left them in a cave with no door on it. So, he told her he'd leave her the rifle and she could shoot anything that tried to come in before he got back. Even so, she was terrified. Which is why Ransom waited until after she fell asleep. He'd be there and back way before she woke up.

He said a quick prayer, quietly put some more wood on the fire, and tiptoed outside.

The moon seemed even a little brighter than last night and because of their little hike this morning, he felt pretty confident about where he was going. The only problem was, and it was a big one, at some point since it got dark it had started to snow. And it was coming down right good. It was already enough to cover his shoes. And the temperature had dropped, too.

Quietly, he made his way back just inside the cave

opening where he'd parked the sled. Pa had reckoned they might see some snow on their journey, so besides insisting he bring their coats, he told Ransom to pack their shoes, his and Ma's, both. Pa's were way too big for Ransom, but Pa said if Ransom kept his shoes on and put them inside Pa's, they'd fit nice and snug and make for some passable boots to wear in the snow.

So, that's what Ransom did, then he went back outside to give them a try. "Well, what do you know?" he whispered aloud. They worked just fine. Ransom buttoned up his father's coat on top of his own, grabbed his rucksack, and headed downhill toward the big house below.

TWENTY MINUTES LATER, Ransom was standing up against the back wall of this huge house, trying to catch his breath. It wasn't just how cold it was, but he had to run—fast as he could—across that clearing between the woods and the house. Through the snow. Without the trees for cover and the moon being so bright, he was just out there in the open for anyone to see.

He waited against that wall for several minutes hoping no one had.

Looked like he was okay. Didn't hear anything but the sound of his own breath. He backed away from the wall and looked up at the place, trying to make sense of it. It was at least twice as tall as their cabin and four times as long. The windows in the bottom half were dark, as were all the windows up above, except one. Right in the middle. It was covered with something, so he couldn't see inside. But it wasn't thick enough to keep all the light from shining through. He didn't see anyone moving about up there, no shadows or anything.

He felt sure about one thing…had to be plenty of food in a house this big. The only question was, how to get inside?

There was a door. He tried that, but it wouldn't open. So, he tried opening the windows. They wouldn't budge, neither. But there was this one by itself on part of a smaller section of the house that stuck out on the left. He tried it, and it moved a little. He kept pushing and pushing. Took a few minutes, but he was finally able to get it open a crack. Enough to fit his fingers inside. He lifted with all his strength, and it started sliding up. He opened it just enough to squeeze through.

Once inside, it took him awhile to see anything. He wasn't sure if this house had electricity. The only light came from what the moon offered through the window. Slowly, his eyes adjusted and certain shapes started to appear. But he couldn't figure out what he was seeing.

He felt a wall to his left, smooth as fine cloth. He let it guide him forward, till he came to another door. This one was unlocked. He stepped inside, to what looked to be the main section of the house. It was still real dark in here, too. But he could see a few more shapes in the shadows. Must be some kind of furniture.

They had some furniture in the cabin, ones Pa had made. But they looked nothing like this. He didn't even know what half these things were made to do. There was a table, big enough to sit ten people. And the top was smooth as glass. He kept moving forward, looking for something that resembled some cabinets or a stove.

Finally, he came to another door. It had no doorknob but it was easy enough to push open, so he did. As he made his way through, he grabbed hold of the wall just inside to steady himself. Felt his hand slide down on something that clicked.

Suddenly, the whole room lit up, bright as the sun. He covered his eyes then tried to find that thing on the wall that clicked to make the light go away. He finally did, and when he clicked it again, the room got dark.

Guess that's electricity.

Was it always that bright? He couldn't imagine it. How could anyone ever get anything done with so much light in their eyes? He waited a few moments, hoping no one else had seen what he'd done.

When it was clear, nothing was happening, he covered his eyes part-way and flicked that thing on the wall again. Again, the whole room lit up. Only this time he was ready. And now he could see why maybe no one had reacted. The room didn't have any windows, but he did see another doorway on the other side.

As he looked around, he also saw what looked like some kind of fancy stove. And all around the room were boxy things he guessed were cabinets. But they weren't nothing like the ones Pa made. So many of them, and so fancy.

What kind of place was this? He wanted so bad to explore but knew he had to hurry. No telling when whoever was upstairs might decide to come down. He decided the first place to check was that doorway, see what was behind it.

CHAPTER 18

When Ransom opened the door, the room was pitch black. He remembered that clicking thing by the other door and felt for one on the wall. He found it, shielded his eyes, and flipped it. Instantly, a light came on though not as bright as the other. And this room was way smaller, surrounded by shelves from floor-to-ceiling. This was the room he needed to find. It was stocked with food.

To be safe, he hurried over to the other clicker-thing and turned the big lights off in the kitchen. Once back inside the food room with the door closed, none of the light escaped. He looked at all the things on the shelves. Lots of boxes of all different sizes. Several rows of jars though nothing like the jars they had back in the cabin. The good thing about jars was, you could see what was inside. He couldn't read what was written on the boxes, but some had drawings or pictures on the cover.

There were also quite a few rows of these odd-looking round things. Like the boxes, they had words written on the front and many had pictures showing different kinds of food. Mostly vegetables and beans. He picked one up that had beans on the front and almost dropped it. Heavier than he expected. Looking it over, he didn't see any way to get it open. It had no lid. Must be some kind of tool folks used to break into it. He put it back on the shelf.

He gathered up a bunch of jars, filled with things he recognized, and put them in his rucksack. He'd have to be real careful with them on the way back to the cave. There was still plenty of room in the sack, so he started looking over the boxes. There was one group all about the same size on a lower shelf. Wasn't sure what they had inside, but the drawings on the front looked like something made for kids. One had a funny looking rabbit with a big smile on his face, looking down into a bowl full of colorful things. Looked like candy to Ransom. Another one had some kind of lion or tiger, smiling and looking at a bowl full of food. Then there was one with two kids staring at a bowl full of brown round things. He had no idea what it was, but they looked pretty happy.

He put all three boxes in his rucksack and was just about to leave when he saw a big jar full of something light brown, on the lower shelf where the boxes were. It also had some happy looking animal next to some great big colorful letters. He wished so bad he could read. He stuck that in the ruck-sack too.

That should be enough. Probably more than they needed. They weren't gonna be in that cave for more than a couple of days. He hadn't told Emma yet, but he figured on coming back out to find some church folks the day after Christmas. Seemed like a better idea, since most folks would be in a happy mood. As he walked back to the door, he turned to give the room one more look over, see if there were anything else he should get.

That's when he saw these two boxes sitting by themselves in the corner. Didn't look like food boxes. They were bigger than the rest and square in shape. Part of him said just to leave them be and start heading back, but another part said to give it a quick look. Maybe just the top one.

There was some writing on the box. Of course, Ransom had no idea what it said. It opened easily, and he looked inside. The first thing he saw was this colorful book with a big Santa Claus standing next to a tree all decorated for Christmas. He knew it had to be Santa from the way Ma described him when she'd tell them stories at Christmas time. The man on the cover looked just the way she told it.

He and Pa used to go out every year and cut down a tree that they'd decorate in the cabin. Of course, it didn't look so fancy as the one on this book, but they always loved it just the same. Sadly, there was no room on the sled to bring the tree decorations with them, the ones they'd made through the years.

Ransom picked the book up and brought it over under the light. He opened it and began turning the pages. There are all kinds of words he couldn't read on each page, but there also lots of colorful drawings like on the cover. It was obviously some kind of storybook. Just looking at the pictures gave him an idea, a way to make this terrible Christmas a little more special for Emma.

Before he felt enough guilt to change his mind, he dropped it in the rucksack. Then he closed the box up the way he found it. Didn't seem to him this book could be all that special to whoever lived in this big place, seeing how they tucked it away in this old box and shoved it in the back of this pantry. At least that's what he told himself as he turned the light off and hurried out the door.

When he got outside, the snow was even deeper. Looked like another few inches had fallen. Thankfully, he could still make out his footprints from the way in, so he followed them back to the cave.

CHAPTER 19

The following morning, Theresa woke up feeling pretty rested. As she glanced at the new alarm clock on her nightstand, she understood why. It was 9:30. She wasn't sure she could call it sleeping in, since she was up so late last night reading a halfway-decent book. Probably didn't get to sleep until after 2 AM. The book wasn't keeping her awake, it was wrestling with memories about today.

Today was Christmas Eve morning.

Reading the non-holiday book helped her squash all the thoughts and feelings of wonderful Christmases past. Before the crash. Like she'd told Bud, maybe someday she'd be able to celebrate Christmas again. Right now, she didn't even want to think about it.

She got out of bed, stretched, and walked to the window. The master bedroom faced the front of the house, and the first thing she noticed was all the new snow that had fallen overnight. Judging by how far it came up to the trees, it was less than a foot. But it was enough to do what Bud had said it would, covered up all his tire tracks from the other day, in the street and her driveway. Once again, she was looking at a winter wonderland.

"Well, thank you Lord for that."

This sprung from some advice her pastor back in New York had given her, the same man who'd suggested she move away to get a fresh start. He'd said, as much as we want our lives on earth to go well and everything to work out, that's not really what the Bible taught. He shared some of the intense hardships many Bible heroes experienced, characters she'd learned about since she was a child. But those Bible stories didn't include any of the things the pastor cited. One after the other. So much suffering and hardship experienced by people who loved God, and clearly, were loved by God.

He'd said, "*Even Jesus said at the Last Supper, in this world we would have many troubles, but be of good cheer, for I have overcome the world.*" Then the pastor said, "*The next day Jesus himself, God's own son, after being tortured and beaten, suffered the worst death imaginable, hanging on a cross.*" The promises God made, the pastor said, were not about a trouble-free life down here. But that he would be with us in our times of trouble and help us get through them, and that he would work all these things — including the troubles and suffering — together for our good.

Theresa stepped away from the window. Funny how the mind works. She had just thanked the Lord for the beautiful scene out her window and, somehow, it took her back to that conversation with her pastor. Probably because that was one of the main things he'd suggested, to try and look for good things that God had done, things she *could* thank Him for, even though—understandably—she wasn't thankful and couldn't comprehend the terrible loss of her family. It would help her see God was still doing good things for her, and help keep her mind from only ever dwelling on her losses.

Did this help? Yeah, sometimes.

She walked back to her bed, grabbed her robe off the bedpost, and headed downstairs for coffee.

Coffee was definitely something she was grateful for.

THERESA DIDN'T MAKE it all the way to the kitchen.

As she walked across the carpet from the stairs around the dining room table she was suddenly aware of something very wrong. From the garage doorway and across the dining room, to the push-through door leading into the kitchen were a set of wet, muddy footprints on the rug.

Her heart started pounding. Someone had been in the house. It had to be sometime last evening or while she'd slept. But whatever the time, she was *in the house* when the intruder broke in. Last evening, she'd gone up to her bedroom fairly early, just after 7:30. Her room was almost as big as her apartment back in Brooklyn. She had a phone up there and a TV, which she could watch from her bed, or from a nice comfy chair in the corner.

How did the thief get in? Even worse, was he still here?

She ran back upstairs and got her gun from the night-stand drawer, then hurried back downstairs. Pressing her ear against the kitchen door, she listened but didn't hear a sound. Carefully, she pushed the door open holding the gun out in front of her. Like she'd seen the cops do on TV. "Please, God, let them be gone." She flicked on the light switch.

The kitchen was empty. She couldn't see any signs that anything had been disturbed. Then again, most thieves didn't steal pots and pans. She pressed her ear against the pantry door but didn't hear a sound. Again, she pushed it open and flicked on the switch. The pantry was empty. Thank God. She headed for the door to the garage and opened it. She looked down at the trail of muddy footprints across the linoleum which led directly to a back window. Once again, no one there.

She set the gun down on the dryer and took a closer look at the window. It was open just a crack. Somehow, she hadn't checked to see if this window had been locked. Clearly, it wasn't. She was about to close it then remembered something from a detective show. Fingerprints. The police always looked for fingerprints. She wasn't sure they did in Black Rock, but they did on TV.

She picked up the gun and headed back toward the kitchen. She thought about looking around downstairs to see what had been stolen, but first she wanted to call Bud and tell him what happened. She was so glad he had given her his phone number.

She set the gun down on the counter, picked up the phone, and dialed Bud's number, hoping he was home. It was Christmas Eve morning, seemed like he could be. The phone rang and rang and rang. Finally, she gave up. She'd have to call the main number for the Sheriff's office. She found it and dialed it, praying it wouldn't be forwarded to Marge.

CHAPTER 20

For the last hour or so, Bud had been down at the office with Andy and Margie doing their little Christmas Eve morning tradition. Margie always brought in an assortment of homemade Christmas cookies. Bud brought the eggnog. Andy brought a homemade apple pie baked by his wife. And, of course, they exchanged presents like most folks do on Christmas morning.

Bud knew this tradition was really because of Andy, him feeling bad that both Bud and Margie lived alone. Tomorrow, Andy would have the traditional Christmas celebration you see in all the movies with his wife and two kids, everyone opening presents around a tree, the big dinner later that day. So, he wanted to do something special for Margie and Bud. Bud was grateful, although by now he was used to being alone on Christmas morning. He'd wake up, eat some of Margie's Christmas cookies and a slice of pie with his coffee, get cleaned up, and head off to church. One of his presents to Andy was letting him take home the rest of the eggnog to share with his family.

A great sacrifice, because Bud loved eggnog.

He was just about ready to head over to the bowl for another when the phone started ringing. Margie got up to answer it. "You stay put, Margie. I'll get it."

"Who'd be calling Christmas Eve morning?" she said.

"Hello, Sheriff's office. Bud speaking."

"Oh, Bud. I'm so glad it's you."

The accent immediately gave away the voice. "Morning, Theresa." He was just about to say *Merry Christmas* but thought better of it.

"I wish it was a good morning." Her voice started breaking, like she was crying.

"Theresa, what's wrong? Are you okay?" He looked over at Margie and Andy, who were now paying attention.

"I guess I'm okay. I'm not hurt, thank God."

"What's the matter? What happened?"

"That thief broke into my house. You know the one you said I didn't have to worry about? Well, guess he figured out how to get across town."

"Oh, no. Theresa, I'm so sorry. How did he get in? He break through a window in the back?"

"He didn't have to. Apparently, I must've left the window in the garage unlocked. He got in through there. First thing I saw when I came downstairs, this row of muddy wet footprints across the dining room carpet."

"What did he take? Can you see anything obvious that's missing?"

"No, not yet. Haven't really looked around to check. I just came downstairs a few minutes ago. When I saw what happened, I went right back up to get my gun. Wanted to make sure he wasn't still in the house. Thankfully, he wasn't. Then I called you."

"Okay, listen, I'll be right over. You should be okay till I get there. This guy never came back to the other two places."

"Well," she said, "he'll be sorry if he does. I'm keeping this gun right next to me till you get here."

"I'll be there quick as I can. While you're waiting, might be a good idea to look around downstairs. Make a list of anything that's missing. That'll help us when we catch him, having a list."

"Okay, I'll do that."

"But do me a favor. If you see anything the thief might have touched, don't disturb the scene. Like drawers pulled out, or by the window he came in at. I want to take some fingerprints, see if it's the same guy."

"Okay. Please, hurry."

Bud hung up and quickly updated Andy and Margie about what happened. They agreed he should leave right away. Andy asked if he wanted him to come along but Bud told him to go home and be with his family. He'd call Andy if anything came up that needed his attention.

But he doubted it would.

HALFWAY THERE, while speeding down the main road on the edge of town, the one that would connect to Elk Hill Road in ten minutes, Bud did something totally stupid. Yes, the roads were covered with almost a foot of snow and the plows had not been out yet. And it looked like Bud had been the first car to drive on this road. But still, this was his town. He'd been down this road a thousand times, knew every twist and turn and hill.

But as he raced around this one blind curve, his rear end got loose and the car started to slide. Bud tried to correct it, but it didn't do any good. The car spun all the way around. Next thing he knew, he had slid off into a ditch. He wasn't hurt, although he wouldn't be surprised if he woke up with some Christmas bruises tomorrow.

The big problem was, and he saw this right off, there was no getting his car out of that ditch without a tow truck. A moment later, it dawned on him. That wasn't the biggest problem. The biggest problem was...he had no way of letting Theresa know why he wouldn't be there in a few minutes, as promised.

He thought about what to do. Seeing as he was at the halfway point, it would take him about as long to walk to Theresa's house, as it would to head back toward town to Jeb's filling station, which was on this road. Jeb had a tow truck, the only tow truck in town. But he knew Jeb's station would be closed, being Christmas Eve. But then, Jeb had a phone booth on the corner of his property. Bud could call him, beg him to come pull his car out of the ditch. Then call Theresa and explain what happened.

Okay, that was the plan. He buttoned up his coat and started the long walk toward Jeb's.

CHAPTER 21

*A*fter fixing her coffee, Theresa had spent the next twenty minutes doing as Bud asked, looking all around the house to see what the thief had stolen. The problem was, it didn't seem like anything was missing. Almost everything in the house was brand-new. Things she had purchased herself and placed in the house herself. So, she would know if something was gone.

Nothing was. How very odd.

Then she noticed something else, something she probably should have seen earlier. There were no muddy footprints anywhere else downstairs, just where she had seen them running from the garage door to the kitchen door. But even in the kitchen, nothing was missing. And there were no drawers pulled out, no mess to clean up.

She walked back to the dining room and looked down at the trail. She followed it into the kitchen, and that's when she saw…the steps led to the pantry. It never dawned on her to look closely in there. She pulled the door open, clicked on the light, and could immediately see…something, several things, were out of place. With so much time on her hands, she'd actually taken great care when stocking the shelves with things from the grocery store. She'd never had a pantry before, so she decided to try to load things in a way that made sense. Things she used all the time in the middle shelves. Things she used less often on the top ones. Heavy things or bigger things on the lowest shelf or the floor.

She stepped inside and began to take a mental inventory. Yes, quite a few things were missing. Bud had asked for a list. She walked back out to the kitchen, grabbed a memo pad and pen on the counter.

The first thing she noticed missing were the jars. Quite a few of them. Pretty much all the jams and jellies were gone. As well as the jars of fruit, like pears, peaches, and cherries. Glancing at the rest of the food in the top and middle shelves, she didn't notice anything else missing. But then she saw a gaping hole in the lower shelf where she stored the cereal boxes. Half of them were gone. Looking over the ones still there, she figured out the stolen ones and wrote them down: *Trix, Frosted Flakes,* and *Cocoa Puffs.* Then she realized, they were all kid cereals.

They were her kids' favorite brands. She didn't just buy them for that reason. Quite a few times she'd eaten them right along with them. They were fun to eat and tasted good.

And now they were gone.

Then she noticed one more thing, something she had stored next to the cereal boxes was also gone. A big jar of JIF peanut butter. After adding it to the list, she stood and examined the shelves one more time. That appeared to be it. Different kinds of food, the only things that were stolen.

Again, how odd.

At least he hadn't taken anything of great value. Less than

ten dollars' worth of food. She wondered what Bud would think about that. Then she realized…where was Bud? She walked back into the kitchen and glanced at the clock. She'd driven into town several times by now, had even driven past the Sheriff's office once. She knew how long it took to get to her place from there. Bud said he was leaving right away. He should have been here by now. Really, over ten minutes ago.

She hoped he was okay.

BUD FINALLY REACHED Jeb's filling station. It was plenty cold out, but he was dressed for it. And the wind had died down to barely a breeze. But he worried what Theresa would think. He should have been there a long time ago.

Oh well, couldn't be helped.

He could tell as he walked up to it, as expected, Jeb's place was closed. There was Jeb's tow truck parked beside his building, partially covered in snow. He knew Jeb's number from memory, from all the times he'd called him for this thing or that. He decided to call Theresa first. Stepping inside the phone booth, he dialed her number and waited as her phone rang.

"Hello?"

"Theresa? It's Bud."

"Bud, I was starting to worry about you. You all right?"

"I'm fine. Sort of." After sharing his embarrassment, he explained what happened with his car.

"You wound up in a ditch? But you weren't hurt?"

"Just my pride. Guess I can't give any more lessons about driving in the snow."

She laughed. "Guess not. But there's a lot more snow out there now than when you gave me my lesson."

"Yeah, I guess. Anyway, it might be a while before I get out there. I'm here at Jeb's filling station. It was the closest place with a phone booth. Obviously, he's not here 'cause of Christmas Eve. I'm going to try to reach him, see if he'll help me out, but I don't know how long that'll take. I could call Andy. I'm sure he'll come get me, drive me out to your place. But he's with his family, and I'm not sure—"

"No, don't call him. Let him enjoy the holiday. I'm doing a lot better now. Like you said, the thief never came back to the places he robbed. So, he probably won't be coming back here. You just come whenever you get your car pulled out of that ditch. I'm not going anywhere."

"Okay, thanks," he said. "Hopefully, it won't be more than an hour or two. Say, were you able to make a list of what was stolen?"

"Yeah, it was pretty strange."

"How so?"

"Nothing valuable was taken. Actually, the only thing he stole was food from my pantry. Certainly nothing expensive."

"That is strange. Definitely not like the other two robberies. But I'm glad, for your sake. Okay, you take care and I'll be there as soon as I can."

THERESA DECIDED to pour herself another cup of coffee. That's when she noticed the light was still on in the pantry. She opened the door to turn it off when something else caught her eye. The top box of the two boxes she'd brought from Brooklyn had been moved. She was something of a neatnik and had set one on top of the other, so that they were perfectly squared. Now, the top box was moved over to the left an inch or so.

Maybe the thief had just bumped into it, but she better make sure. She opened it up, looked inside, and gasped.

"It's gone," she said aloud. "I can't believe it. It's gone." She bent down and moved several things around to make sure it hadn't just slid to one of the sides. But it hadn't. It was definitely not there.

Tears filled her eyes. The thief could have stolen anything else in the house, no matter how expensive, compared to this, she wouldn't have cared. But he had taken the one thing she had left from her old place that could never be replaced.

The little children's storybook that Tom used to read to the kids every night before Christmas and, finally, on Christmas Eve. She couldn't believe they had taken it.

"Oh, Lord. Why this? Anything else but this."

CHAPTER 22

*I*t was lunchtime in the cave. And for the first time in a long time, Ransom couldn't wait.

Emma was playing with her dolls, closer to the fire. Earlier that morning when she woke up, she could hardly believe the food Ransom had laid out on the rucksack. "You got all this from that big house?" she'd said.

"You wouldn't believe how much more I left behind," he'd replied. "A whole room full, shelf after shelf."

The harder part was figuring out what it all was. She'd asked him which ones were for breakfast and which ones were for lunch. He had no idea. So, he told her since it was Christmas Eve morning, she could pick whatever caught her fancy. Without hesitating, she went for the box with the kids looking at a bowlful of round, brown things. Ransom had to open it for her. They had no bowls, so after rinsing her hands in the canteen water, Ransom let her eat with her hands.

After putting one fist full in her mouth, her face lit up. He hadn't seen her eyes so wide and bright since he didn't know when.

"You like it, huh?" he said.

She had just nodded and kept eating, handful after handful. He'd finally tried some himself. A wonderful flavor he'd never tasted before seemed to explode in his mouth. But it was strange, as soon as you chewed these little round things it was like they disappeared. But you didn't care, because it tasted so good. He was half-tempted to just eat that, but he had his eyes on that jar of pears.

Emma had stopped eating long enough to say, "Now, I know why the kids on the box look so happy."

Since then, Emma contented herself with her dolls while Ransom tended to the fire and continued to carve her Christmas present. She'd been so distracted by the new food, she hadn't even asked him when they were going down the hill and try to find some city folk. He was glad. He knew she'd be sad when he told her he felt they should wait till at least one day after Christmas. But then, with all this fun food to eat, maybe she wouldn't care.

"Hey, Emma. It's time for lunch, if not way past."

She looked up at him, a big smile on her face. "Can I have more of what I had for breakfast?"

"If you want, but maybe you might want to try what's in those other two boxes. The kids on those look pretty happy, too."

SEVERAL HOURS HAD PASSED, and it was now late afternoon. Theresa had just received one of several calls from Bud, updating her on his progress. Or, the lack thereof. The problem was, apparently, getting a hold of Jeb. Each time Bud had called her, he was so apologetic and clearly felt terrible for making her wait so long. Theresa was able to reassure him she was doing much better now. And that he could just get there whenever he was able. She had her gun. And her TV.

That last call was Bud saying he was finally on his way.

This time, it turned out to be true. Ten minutes later, she heard him pull into the driveway.

She hurried to the door to unlock it and be ready to open it as soon as he knocked. She watched as he walked across the front of the house through the snow toward the front door. When she heard him banging his boots on the porch, she opened it. "Come on in. It's nice and warm in here."

"Good," he said. "I could use some warm."

After he stepped inside, she quickly closed the door. "Sorry, you had such a hard time."

"I'm sorry I did, too. But mostly for stringing you along all afternoon."

"That's okay. You're here now. You want some hot coffee?"

"Please. Hot anything."

She hung his coat up on the coat rack, and he followed her to the kitchen.

"The place looks just the same," he said.

"Yeah, for some reason, looks like the thief didn't even try to take anything in the living or dining area. He just went right for the pantry."

"That really is strange. You got some really nice stuff in here."

She poured him a cup and refilled her own. "Doesn't feel like mine yet. The house, either, for that matter."

"I guess that won't happen until you start making some new memories here."

She handed him the cup. "Well, this is certainly going to be one. My first Christmas Eve robbery."

He laughed. "Well, glad it was only some food."

She'd told him about that on one of his earlier calls but didn't mention the stolen Christmas book. Maybe she should now. "Actually, the thief did take one thing besides food." She paused, sensing her emotions rising. "Probably the thing I care about most in this house. More than any of this nice stuff." There it went, a tear slid down her cheek. She quickly wiped it on her sleeve.

"I'm so sorry. What was it?"

"Nothing expensive. Just, it meant a whole lot..." She pointed to her heart. "...in here." She told him all about the book, what their tradition was, and why it meant so much to her. As more tears flowed, he walked over, grabbed a napkin, and handed it to her.

"Well, Theresa. I'm almost positive we'll get that book back. All the other things the thief stole were things he could sell for money. But clearly, he didn't take that book to sell it. Couldn't get very much for a well-used children's book."

"I hope so. But speaking of resale value...it's not as if he could get anything for the food he stole, either. Whoever he is, he must not be doing very well. To break into a place just to steal food."

"Yeah," Bud said. "That part of it doesn't make very much sense. Had a lot of time to think this afternoon. This whole thing doesn't quite add up with the other two. There are so many houses over by where the other two robberies took place. All of them have kitchens. If he was hungry, why didn't he take some of their food?"

"Yeah," she said. "That is strange. Drive all the way over

here, break into one of the biggest houses in town, and only take some food out of the pantry? Then there's the list of things he stole. I didn't tell you this part. Several boxes of kids' cereal. A bunch of jars of fruit, and big jar of JIF peanut butter."

"Really? That's all the food he took?"

She nodded. "That's it. That…and my Christmas book."

He set his coffee cup down. "Could you show me which window he came in at?"

"I will, but talking about food…did you even get to eat lunch?"

"Well, no. Had to skip it. Really wasn't any—"

"I thought so. C'mon. This investigation can wait a little while longer. You gotta eat. I can heat up the leftover spaghetti and meatballs we had the other night."

"That sounds amazing."

"Tom always said my spaghetti actually tasted better as leftovers."

Just over an hour later, after a wonderful dinner and some great conversation, Bud looked outside. It was getting dark. Theresa had just finished telling the story about how she and Tom had discovered Black Rock during their honeymoon. "Theresa, I really would love to keep talking, but…I gotta do something outside before it gets too dark to see. It's already almost there."

"Oh, yeah. Sure. You wanted me to show you where the thief got in. I'll do that, you go outside, do whatever you gotta do. I'll clean up a little."

Theresa walked him through the dining room and into the laundry room section of the garage. She pointed to a window. "It's this one here. I haven't touched it, in case you want to dust it for prints."

"Thanks. I probably will. But first, I want to check out another kind of prints." He glanced out the window. "Okay, there they are." Looking back at her. "See 'em? The footprints in the snow?" He looked out the window again. "I better run out to my car and grab my flashlight."

CHAPTER 23

*J*t took Theresa about fifteen minutes to get things clean enough to where she could leave them for the morning. She walked back to the dining room and looked out the back window. No sign of Bud. He said he wanted to check out the footprints in the snow. How long could that take? By now, it was totally dark outside. She went into the laundry room and turned on the outside light then looked out the window from there. She saw two sets of footprints leading from the window out toward the woods.

She hoped he was okay. "Lord, let him be all right." He was obviously tracking the prints of the thief. She guessed the path must have led deeper into the woods. What if he met the guy and got hurt in some kind of confrontation? Should she call the sheriff? She decided maybe she should put her coat on first and go to the edge of the woods, call out his name a few times. If he didn't respond, she'd come back and call for help.

After grabbing her flashlight from the junk drawer, she grabbed her big coat in the front door closet, put on her boots, and headed for the back door. As she opened it and turned on the flashlight, she started to doubt whether this was a smart thing to do. If the thief had been able to get the better of Bud, what chance did she have if he started coming back to the house? Maybe, she should go get her gun and wait right here.

Just then, she saw a light flickering through the trees. Was it Bud...or the thief?

She was about to go back for her gun when she flashed her light toward the edge of the woods and saw Bud coming out of the trees. He looked up, smiled, and waved at her.

Okay, he was fine. That's all that mattered. She flashed at him again and realized he wasn't just waving at her, he was gesturing that she should come join him. What in the world was going on? But she did as he asked and headed his way.

When she got closer, he said excitedly, "Theresa, I'm glad you came out. I was just coming back to get you. You gotta see this."

"See what? Did you find the thief?"

"Yeah," he said. "But it's not at all what I expected. When I first saw those footprints in the snow, I got worried that it was the same thief as the other two robberies. The boot size looked just the same. But in the other two, the footprints led to the side of the house and out toward the street. These just disappeared into the woods. But because of the snow, I was able to follow them right to where the thieves—if you could call them that — were staying."

"Did you say *thieves*, plural?"

He laughed. "Yeah, but it's okay. I'd rather show you what I found, if you don't mind. Come on, follow me." He started heading back toward the woods.

"You want to take me to where the thieves are hiding?"

"Yeah, but trust me. There's no danger. You really need to see this."

So, she followed.

ABOUT TEN MINUTES LATER, after a fairly steep uphill climb, they reached a place where the ground leveled off. Bud had told her they were heading for a cave and as soon as they reached it, he'd be turning off his flashlight. They needed to be very quiet.

His flashlight had just gone off. He reached for her hand and said, "Just want to make sure you don't trip."

She found that she didn't mind this at all. After a dozen or more steps, her eyes adjusted to the dimmer light. She could now see another big hill rising up to the right and in the middle of the shadows, a flickering light revealed the edges of the cave.

He stopped and whispered, "They're just kids, Theresa. A boy and a little girl. All by themselves. Pretty sure it's a brother and sister. After about ten or fifteen feet, the cave jogs to the right. That's where they are, sitting by a fire. I stood there watching them for a few minutes until I realized what was going on. After that, I decided to come get you instead of going in there by myself."

"What can I do?" she asked.

"First, I just want you to see the situation for yourself. Then we'll let the kids know we're there. I just thought it would go better if they saw a woman first, instead of someone in a uniform."

"Okay, if that's what you think's best. You go on. I'm right behind you."

He continued to hold her hand as they entered the cave.

With her other hand she felt the cold stone wall. A few steps more, the light from the fire inside grew brighter on the cave walls. Now she could hear a little boy's voice. Sounded like he was telling some kind of story.

A moment later, Bud stopped and whispered very quietly, "Come around me until you're close beside me. I want you to see this. But be very quiet." He let go of her hand.

She came around beside him and could now see into the bigger area of the cave on the right. The scene she saw, and heard, totally melted her heart.

A little boy — couldn't be much older than her Tommy — was sitting by the fire. Tucked in next to him wrapped in a blanket was a little girl. The boy was holding Theresa's book, her special Christmas book: *The Night Before Christmas*. To his left, spread out on some kind of canvas bag, were all the stolen food items from her pantry. The boy was obviously reading the story to the little girl.

Theresa listened, and as she did, her eyes filled with tears.

Okay, I'll tell it to you one more time, Emma. But that's the last time. Don't matter that it's Christmas Eve, you gotta get to sleep, else Santa won't come and bring you your present.

All right, the little girl said. *Just one more time then.*

Okay.

He opened to the first page.

One snowy night, kinda like tonight, there was this big house, kinda like the house where I got this book and all this good food. And it was Christmas Eve, just like tonight.

He turned the page.

And inside this big house was the finest Christmas tree you ever saw, inside the biggest room you ever saw. The whole room was decorated for Christmas.

He turned to the next page.

The children were all in their beds, the nicest beds you ever saw. And all of them were thinking about one thing...all the candy they would get for Christmas the next day. See, here's the picture showing the very thing.

He showed her the picture then turned the page.

The Ma and Pa were asleep in their bed, the biggest bed you ever saw, when the Pa heard something outside. He got up right quick.

He turned the page again.

He opened that window and looked all around but couldn't see nothing.

But that's when he heard Santa and the reindeers, the little girl said. *Right?*

He turned to the next page.

That's right. Up on a hill nearby, was old Santa himself. Sitting in the biggest sleigh, plum full of toys. The reindeer all out in front, bells jingling around their collars.

"Do you see what's going on?" Bud whispered to Theresa.

She nodded, wiped the tears from her eyes. "He can't read. He's just describing the pictures on the page. Oh, Bud, what's going on here?"

"Can't be sure till we talk to 'em. But I think they're mountain kids, orphans most likely."

"We have to help them," she said. "What can we do?"

"Let's go in. You first, so they see you first. But I'll do the talking. You feel free to jump in whenever you want."

"All right. I'm ready."

Theresa got in front of Bud, and the two of them stepped into the bigger room closer to the fire. For a moment, the little boy kept telling his story. Then the children both looked up and saw them.

"It's all right kids," Bud said in a pleasant voice. "We're not here to hurt you."

"It's the law," the little girl screamed, and buried her face into the boy's side.

The little boy's eyes were full of terror and fear. He looked over at the food, set the book down, then looked up at Theresa. "This your food we stole, Ma'am? And this here book?"

"Yes," she said, "those are my things, but—"

"I only took 'em cause we had no food left. You can have it all back. We only ate a little. And the book, too. Just wanted to do something nice for Emma."

"Is Emma your sister?" Theresa said softly, trying to smile.

"Yes, Ma'am. She's five. My name's Ransom." He looked at Bud. "You here to take us to jail, sir?"

Bud came around and stood beside Theresa. "No, Ransom. I'm not taking anyone to jail tonight."

"Why are you children here in this cave?" Theresa said. "Where are your parents?"

Ransom's eyes shifted from fear to sadness. "Ma died a few years back. Pa died just a few weeks back. Coughing something fierce, just like our Ma, till the end. We lived in a cabin quite a few days back in the woods." Tears rolled down his cheeks. "Pa made me promise to take Emma here and go find some city folk. We only been in this cave a day. I was planning to do that but wanted to wait till after Christmas."

"Oh, Bud," Theresa grabbed Bud's sleeve, buried her face in it. "These poor children."

"I know we done wrong, Ma'am," Ransom said. He looked at Bud. "But please don't split us apart. Whatever else you gotta do, please don't do that. Pa made me promise that I'd—"

"We're not going to split you apart," Bud said. "Not for now, anyway."

Theresa pulled away from Bud, stepped closer to the children, and bent down. "No one is going to split you apart." The tears came again. "Not now, and not ever. Not if I can help it." She looked back at Bud, who smiled. She wiped her tears away. "And I don't care that you took my food, or that book. You're welcome to all that, and anything else I got in my big old house. Which is where you both are going to sleep tonight. I've got some of the biggest beds you ever saw. That's where you're going to spend Christmas Eve. With me. And you won't need a fire to keep warm."

"She's got electricity, Emma," Ransom said, smiling for the first time.

Theresa laughed. "That's right. I've got electricity. And you're welcome to it. Both of you."

Emma finally pulled her face out from Ransom's side and looked at Theresa, then up at Bud.

"Are you...church folk?" she said.

Theresa laughed again, looked back at Bud, then at Emma. "Yes, Emma. We're church folk. Now, are you two ready to come home with me?"

They stood up. "Yes, Ma'am, " Ransom said. "I believe we are."

CHAPTER 24

As they made their way out of the cave, Ransom asked Bud what he should do with the fire. Bud told him not to worry about it. It would burn itself out. He then asked him to put all the food back in his canvas bag. "And don't forget the Christmas book." He walked over to Emma, squatted down, and said, "Are you okay with me carrying you through the woods back to the house? I don't want you to fall and get hurt."

"Okay, sir. I don't want to fall, neither." She reached up for him, and he scooped her up in one arm. "Wait, I forgot somethin'."

He put her down. She ran into the cave and came back with a rough-looking doll and something like a doll made of sticks. "Okay," she said. "Now, we can go."

Seeing this, Ransom said, "I better check something, too." He dug through his sack till he pulled out a small box. "Okay...Pa's soldiers." He placed the box back in the sack. "How will we see in these woods? Moon's mostly covered by clouds."

"Don't worry," Theresa said. "We've got flashlights."

"What's a flashlight?" he asked.

Theresa looked at Bud then back at Ransom. She held hers out. "It's this. You just click the switch, and the light comes on. Like this."

Both he and Emma gasped.

"When you want to turn it off, just click the switch the other way."

"Could I try it?" he said.

"Sure. In fact, why don't you lead the way back to my house? Just shine down on the ground and follow our footprints."

Bud turned his on, too.

Ransom held the flashlight and clicked it on. "Emma, you seeing this?" He turned around and pointed it at her. She and Bud quickly covered their eyes. Ransom lowered it back to the ground. "I'm sorry. I didn't mean to—"

"It's okay, Ransom," Theresa said. "You just need to remember, never shine it in anyone's face."

"Okay. I'm sorry." He pointed it back to the ground and found the path of footprints. "Are we ready?"

"We are," Bud said. "Lead the way."

After walking a few moments, Ransom said, "With something like this, you could do anything you want to at night. Anything at all."

Theresa never imagined so much wonder could be found in a flashlight.

As soon as they were back to the house, Theresa said to Bud, "We have to give these kids a bath. First thing."

"I agree. I'm gonna take a guess, they've never seen a

modern bathroom. How do you want to do this?" He set Emma down. "Obviously, you're going to need to take care of Emma. She should probably go first."

"They don't have to take turns. I've got two bathrooms upstairs. One in the hall and another one in my bedroom."

"Wow," he said. "Both have tubs?"

"And showers. But I think we should use the tubs."

While they talked, the children were just looking around the downstairs, awestruck by the sight. Even Ransom, but then Theresa realized when he had come here to get the food, all the lights were probably off. "Ransom, do you and Emma have any pajamas? You know, night clothes?"

"We do, Ma'am. Got it right here in my sack. We haven't wore 'em since we left the cabin. It was so cold every night, we just stayed in our clothes."

"Does that mean they're clean?"

"Yes, Ma'am. Washed them myself."

"Is that all the clothes you have?" she said. "The ones you're wearing and the ones for nighttime?"

"Pretty much," he said. "Have a few more things back at the cabin, but didn't have room to bring 'em on my sleigh."

"Okay, that's okay. We'll just use the ones in your sack for tonight. You understand what Bud and I were talking about? Giving you and Emma baths?"

"I think so. You wanna clean us up?"

Theresa said yes and went on to explain — as simply as she could — what was going to happen. The thing that Ransom marveled at the most was the idea that no one had to heat the water up on the stove.

FORTY-FIVE MINUTES LATER, both children were all cleaned

up and had changed into their night clothes. Theresa almost cried when she saw what they had to wear. But she did her best not to react. The house had five bedrooms, and she had fully furnished three of them, including hers. Thinking that at some point her family from Brooklyn would come down to visit. She had initially said they both could have their own room but Ransom quickly saw the look on his sister's face, and asked if they could please sleep in the same room. He even volunteered to sleep on the floor.

Theresa said, "You don't have to do that, Ransom. One of the rooms has two beds in it. You can both sleep in that room."

"Thank you much, Ma'am. Y'all been so kind to us. Now I know why Pa said to be sure to find some church folk."

She glanced at a clock on the wall. "Really should get you kids to bed. It's getting late. Did you have any dinner?"

"We ate plenty. Not like any dinner we ever had," Emma said.

"Never tasted food like...well, like the food in your pantry," said Ransom.

"I saw you picked the kid cereals. You ever had cereal with milk?"

"No, Ma'am."

"Well, you're in for a real treat then. You can have some tomorrow morning." Then she suddenly remembered. Tomorrow was Christmas morning. She looked over the banister at the living area below. Not a single holiday thing in sight. She remembered that one little box of Christmas items in the pantry. They were mostly little personal things and couldn't begin to help decorate a room this size. She looked over at Bud, who seemed to quickly grasp what she was thinking.

"Too bad it's Christmas Eve," he said. "All the stores are closed."

She sighed. "Okay, well let's get you two kids into bed." She walked down the hall and led them into the bedroom with two beds. She pulled down the bedspread, blankets, and sheets, fluffed up the pillows, and said, "Okay, jump in."

Ransom quickly did but Emma needed help to get into hers. As she tucked her little body under the blankets and laid her head back on the pillow, her eyes got big and wide. "This is just like the bed Ransom talked about in that Christmas story." She looked over at her brother. "Isn't it, Ransom?"

"I ain't never been in a bed this big or this soft," he said. "I'm afraid I go to sleep, I won't ever wake up."

Again, Theresa was struck with how she had never given two thoughts about the comforts of a good bed.

"Excuse me, Ma'am," Emma said. "Do you know how to read words?"

"I do. Why?"

"Do you think…it being Christmas Eve, and all. Could you read us them words in that storybook Ransom was reading before? The ones with the kids in a house like this, then Santa comes?"

Theresa took a deep breath. How could she say no?

"I know right where it is," Bud said from the doorway. "I'll be right back."

CHAPTER 25

en minutes later, Bud was standing in the doorway watching one of the most touching things he had seen in a good long while. She had let Ransom hop into Emma's bed while she read the story aloud. Both kids had snuggled up close to her, so they could see the pictures while she read the words.

"Okay, kids. I'm gonna start at the beginning." She looked down at Ransom. "I heard you telling the story to Emma in the cave. You did a pretty good job guessing without knowing the words. But here's what they actually say. It's a very special story.

'Twas the night before Christmas, when all through the house
Not a creature was stirring, not even a mouse.
The stockings were hung by the chimney with care
In hopes that Saint Nicholas soon would be there.

SHE TURNED THE PAGE. "Saint Nicholas is another name for Santa."

. . .

THE CHILDREN WERE NESTLED all snug in their beds,
  While visions of sugarplums danced in their heads.
  And Mama in her 'kerchief, and I in my cap,
  Had just settled our brains for a long winter's nap.

WHEN OUT ON the roof there arose such a clatter,
  I sprang from my bed to see what was the matter.

BUD WATCHED as the children sat mesmerized by what Theresa read, thinking about how bad she was feeling that she had nothing to give them tomorrow. Not a single present. And her home would look nothing like the story.

Suddenly, an amazing idea popped into his head.

"Excuse me, kids, Theresa. Hate to interrupt you. But I just thought of something I need to do. Something very important."

"You're leaving?" Theresa said. "Where? Back out in the snow?"

"Yeah, but I'll—"

"Do you have to leave right now?"

"I do, but if everything works out, I should be back here in about an hour. Might be sooner but gonna have to drive extra special slow."

"Oh, good. Okay, whatever it is, please be careful."

"I will. But you kids, I'm sure you'll be asleep by the time I get back. So, I'll see you in the morning. Merry Christmas." He took off toward the stairs.

"Merry Christmas!" he heard all three of them yell back.

. . .

IT TOOK Bud more like an hour and a half to get back to Theresa's place. But he was able to call her thirty minutes ago to let her know he was running a little late. Not surprisingly, he didn't see another car on the road all the way there and back. His car was completely loaded, even the roof. He was just about to go in and ask her to help him bring everything into the house.

Then he thought better of it.

It was a risk, for sure, what he was thinking about doing, but after seeing how Theresa responded to the children from the moment she entered that cave until he'd left to run his errand, it was a risk he was willing to take.

He got out of the car and retraced his footprints in the snow back to her porch. He didn't want to ring the bell or knock loudly in case the kids were already asleep. After banging the snow off his boots he knocked gently two times, then let himself in. He could hear her making some noise in the kitchen. He walked over toward the door and called out her name. Figured, if he'd just gone in he might've scared her to death.

She quickly came out. "Bud, you're back."

"Sorry, thought I should let myself in." He explained why.

"That's fine. So, what was this big important thing you had to do? Thought you probably didn't want to say upstairs, because it has something to do with the kids. They're both fast asleep, by the way."

"It did have something to do with the kids, why I left I mean. But now I'm thinking, it also has something to do with you."

"Something to do with me? What is it?"

"It's a surprise. It'll spoil it if I tell you."

"A surprise?" She smiled.

"Yeah. Kind of a big one. But you're going to have to trust me a little. Well, maybe more than a little."

"Trust you for what?"

"Well, I'm gonna need you to go upstairs, like now...for the night. And stay upstairs until tomorrow morning."

Her smile got bigger. "What are you thinking? What did you do?"

"I can't tell you. You'll see it tomorrow. Right now, I need you to do what I ask." He tried to say this playfully. "And don't come down until morning. For the next hour or so, I'll be making some noise down here. But you can't peek."

She shook her head. "All right. Guess I'll have to trust you then. Let me just go finish up in the kitchen. Won't take two minutes."

CHAPTER 26

 hristmas Morning

WHEN THERESA AWOKE, it took her a few moments to remember the amazing events of the night before. And that two little children were fast asleep in one of her guest bedrooms. And that today was Christmas. And that Bud had asked her to stay up here in her room…until now.

What was this big surprise?

She put on her robe, opened her bedroom door, and wondered what to expect. The first thing she realized, there wasn't a sound coming from the children's room. She walked to the banister overlooking the downstairs and could not believe the scene below.

"Oh, my goodness."

It was incredible.

It was like looking at a picture right out of the storybook. A fully decorated Christmas tree, all lit up, stood just to the left of her fireplace, which was burning nicely. At least ten wrapped Christmas presents were spread out beneath its branches.

Bud had even hung stockings across the fireplace mantle.

As she came down the stairs to look closer, she saw Bud sound asleep in his clothes, less his boots, on her sofa.

What a wonderful man he was. She walked over to the presents and saw half had Ransom's name written on them, and Emma's name on the other half.

Bud woke up. "Good morning," he said, stretching. "Merry Christmas."

She walked closer, resisting an urge to hug him. "Bud, how did you do all this? It was Christmas Eve. You said all the stores were closed. I don't under—"

"It's from my church," he said. "Or...church folk, as the kids would call it." He sat up and explained.

He remembered his pastor saying they had collected way too many toys for the needy this year. They had already passed out ones to all the folks in town having hard times, and he wasn't sure what to do with the rest. And the church had this beautiful tree all done up in the lobby. So, Bud called him, told him all about the kids they'd found in the woods, and without hesitation the pastor had said, *"By all means, Bud. You go get that stuff and bring it to those kids. Even the tree. I'll explain things to the congregation at the Christmas service in the morning."*

Bud stood, pointed to everything and said, "So, here it is. Isn't it something? First time I ever got a chance to play Santa."

"Bud, it's...it's just..." She was starting to tear up.

"You're not mad? I was hoping I was reading you right last night."

"No, I'm not mad. It's…it's beautiful." She couldn't help it. She had to hug him. After a moment, he hugged back.

She pulled away, looked up and said, Let's go right up and wake the kids."

"Want me there, too?"

"Of course, I want you there, too."

And so, they did. Took the kids a few minutes to realize where they were, but they quickly followed Bud and Theresa to the stairs. When they saw the scene below, Emma screamed, "Look Ransom, he came! Santa came!" She ran down the stairs.

Ransom didn't follow. He turned, his eyes full of tears, and ran to Theresa, giving her the biggest hug. "Thank you, thank you, thank you," he said. "For everything."

"You're welcome," Theresa said. "Merry Christmas." She looked over at Bud and silently said, "Thank you."

Ransom finally let go, so she said, "Go on, Ransom. Looks like Santa left quite a few presents for you under the tree."

"For me?"

She nodded. "You and Emma. Go see."

He ran down the stairs.

Bud walked toward her, whispered. "We better get down there and help."

She was confused. "Why?"

"I wrote their names on the presents…but they can't read. Remember?"

"You're right. I forgot. Let's go."

As they headed down the stairs, she said, "I'm gonna have to fix that right away."

BUD STOOD at the bottom of the steps, taking in the scene. He was exhausted, but he didn't care. He couldn't recall ever having a finer Christmas morning than this. And it was amazing to see how Theresa responded to the moment, how quickly she seemed to set aside the deep personal feelings he knew she must have, to care for two children she'd only just met.

She really was something special.

EPILOGUE

4 Weeks Later

WHAT HAD HAPPENED WITH THERESA, Bud, and the two orphaned children over the Christmas holiday had been the talk of the town. For the most part, Bud thought, in a good way.

It didn't hurt that the way this information had gotten out to the public didn't come from anything Bud, Andy, or even Margie had said. It came from the pastor's sermon on Christmas morning.

Bud didn't hear about it firsthand. He'd stayed there at Theresa's to help her with Ransom and Emma all morning. Margie had filled him in after she got home from church. Apparently, until the pastor got up to speak everyone was buzzing about who'd stolen the church's Christmas tree and all the presents underneath.

Wisely, he'd begun his sermon drawing everyone's attention to the big empty spot on stage, then reassured them these things had not been stolen, but that he—on their behalf —had given them away for "the best of reasons." Before sharing any of the details, he had them turn to the text in Luke where Mary and Joseph discovered they have to deliver the baby Jesus in a stable, because *"there was no room for them in the inn."*

He'd said that was going to be his text anyway that morning, but in light of what had happened the night before, it had taken on a new air of relevance and significance for him, and he wanted to share why. The pastor went on to explain who Theresa was, the tragedy she'd experienced in her own life two Christmases ago, and how inspired he was by her response when these two orphaned mountain kids showed up on her doorstep that night.

She not only had *not* turned them away—as the innkeeper had done—she set aside her grief and opened both her door and her heart wide to let them in. He closed his sermon reading that passage in Matthew where Jesus talks about caring for the poor and needy, and said, *"Whatever you do for the least of these brothers of mine, you do unto Me."* Margie said there wasn't a dry eye in the house as they sang the closing Christmas hymn.

Needless to say, in the weeks that followed it seemed the entire town of Black Rock had taken Ransom and Emma into their hearts. Theresa repeatedly told Bud how overwhelmed she was by the way folks treated her, with so much kindness and support.

And she had just received some wonderful news by the State Office for Child Welfare. After reviewing the report submitted by the lady they'd sent to investigate the matter, they unanimously approved her being named as foster parent and legal guardian for Ransom and Emma.

Bud asked her did she have any thoughts about the long-term situation and, before he'd even finished his question, she said in her finest Brooklyn accent: "Bud, these kids aren't going nowhere."

But to Bud, maybe the best part of the story was how much she seemed to be warming up to him. When he worked up the courage to ask if she'd ever considered him and her, you know, did she ever "think of him *that way.*" She smiled and said, "Only all the time." But then added she just wasn't quite ready yet for that step.

"Take all the time you need, Theresa," he said. "Like those kids, I'm not going anywhere, either."

A NOTE TO MY READERS

I hope you enjoyed reading *Twas The Night*. While not part of a series, I've written similar full-length novels that are also set during the holiday season, such as *The Unfinished Gift* and *The Reunion* (You can find these books on Amazon, also on Kindle and Kindle Unlimited).

I've also written more suspenseful novels like *The Discovery*, *What Follows After*, or my *Jack Turner Suspense Series*. If you go to Amazon and Search "Dan Walsh Books" you'll see I've written more than 25 novels. All of them are there, all are available in Print, Kindle, and most are on Kindle Unlimited also.

I should mention *Twas The Night* is entirely a work of fiction, although the plane crash over New York City at the beginning really did happen. To learn more, look up the "Park Slope Plane Crash" on Google or YouTube.

How You Can Help Me to Keep Writing Novels

If you enjoyed *Twas The Night*, PLEASE consider leaving a

brief review on Amazon. It's the best gift you can give any author and—more than anything—helps readers decide which books to read next.

I'm convinced my readers' willingness to leave reviews for my books have made a major difference in my ability to write full time, and to keep doing it in the years to come.

All you have to do is go on Amazon, search for this book, then scroll down to where it says "Customer Reviews." Below that is a Button that says: "Write A Customer Review."

It's that easy. Thanks in Advance!

Dan Walsh

ABOUT THE AUTHOR

Dan was born in Philadelphia in 1957. His family moved down to Daytona Beach, Florida in 1965, when his father began to work with GE on the Apollo space program. That's where Dan grew up.

He married Cindi, the love of his life in 1976. They have 2 grown children and 5 grandchildren. Dan served as a pastor for 25 years then began writing fiction full-time in 2010. His bestselling novels have won numerous awards, including 3 ACFW Carol Awards (he was a finalist 6 times) and 4 Selah Awards. Four of Dan's novels were finalists for RT Reviews' Inspirational Book of the Year. One of his novels, *The Reunion*, is being made into a major full-length feature film.